RYA   Ryan, Kendall, author.
      Finding Alexei

8/2019   FRA

Finding ALEXEI

New York Times & USA Today Bestselling Author

KENDALL RYAN

D1713796

ST. MARY PARISH LIBRARY
FRANKLIN, LOUISIANA

Finding Alexei
Copyright © 2018 Kendall Ryan

Content Editing by
Elaine York

Copy Editing by
Pam Berehulke

Cover Design and Formating by
Uplifting Designs

All rights reserved. No part of this book may be
reproduced or transmitted in any form without
written permission of the author, except by a
reviewer who may quote brief passages for review
purposes only.

This book is a work of fiction. Names, characters,
places, and incidents are either the product of the
author's imagination or are used fictitiously.

ST. MARY PARISH LIBRARY
FRANKLIN, LOUISIANA

About the Book

He's bossy, moody, and overprotective.

He's also a pro athlete who needs to focus on winning games and staying out of the headlines.

I'm fiercely independent and need a man like I need a second period each month.

So when our worlds collide, I never expected him to be the one to jump in and save me. Especially not when my ex-roommate disappears, leaving me with her baby.

I'm clueless about babies—and it shows. Good thing Alexei isn't. With six nieces and nephews and an apparent hero complex, the dude is both sexy and more than capable. It's a combination that makes it easy to forget we're just playing house.

CHAPTER One

Alexei

S he's petite yet curvy with a nice ass and beautiful tits. But that's not the first thing I notice about her.

The first thing that strikes me is that her coat isn't warm enough for a Chicago winter.

It's dark out, and barely above freezing. She's standing on a street corner discussing something with a man in hushed tones, waving her hands dramatically as she speaks. It's nearly midnight, and the street is almost deserted.

She has long dark hair, a trim build, and a full pouty mouth. And she seems to be pissed off. Curious about her, I stalk closer and then slow my pace.

"Fine. Tell me what it'll take, sweetheart," the guy says to her.

She stiffens and puts one hand on her hip. "I'm not for sale, asshole. I did my job, but that's it. When you step outside those doors, the fantasy ends."

They're standing outside a dingy club, the kind of place that smells of rancid smoke, cheap beer, and meaningless sex. I should know. I've been here once or twice for bachelor parties and those kinds of things. My friends would call it a titty bar. But my friends are mostly pro football players, and their manners leave a lot to be desired.

The place isn't really a strip club, more like a topless bar where beautiful women serve drinks in their underwear. It all seemed innocent enough, until now . . . until a sinking feeling washes over me as I watch this woman get propositioned in the street as she's trying to leave work.

The guy laughs, the sound abrasive, like he doesn't believe her. "Three hundred bucks. Come on, baby. It'll be fast."

She chews on one of those pouty lips as she weighs his words, contemplating what looks to be a life-changing decision . . . and not life-changing in a positive way.

Don't do it, lady . . . just say no to what this asshole is offering you.

Part of me knows I need to mind my own damn business, that this guy just wants a quick fuck. Who am I to judge how this woman chooses to support herself? The other part of me—the fierce protector in me—says this is a situation that I can't ignore. I won't allow this asshole to force a woman to do something she's not comfortable with.

I walk over, my legs moving of their own volition.

"Excuse me," I say, interrupting them.

Her gaze swings over to mine, and the guy she's with does a double-take. I tower over him by at least half a foot. Now that I have a better look at him, I see the guy is middle-aged, round in the midsection, his hair graying at his temples. I also know I can take him if it comes to that.

He shoots me a look that's half pissed off that I interrupted his bargaining session, and half panicked that I may kick his ass. The latter is definitely what he should be more concerned about if he tries any shit. I may just decide to do it anyway, despite the fact I just promised my agent I'll behave myself and not end up on any more tabloid news sites.

"The lady said to leave her alone. I suggest you get the fuck out of here." I glare down at the guy.

His eyes narrow, but he takes a step back and holds up his palms. "Fine. Going."

He takes off down the street and disappears around the corner, leaving me standing across from the woman. She's probably no more than five foot three, a hundred twenty pounds soaking wet. No way she could have defended herself against someone his size. More importantly, she shouldn't have to defend herself from that prick.

"Were you really going to go home with that guy?"

She shakes her head. "No. He didn't want to take me home. Just wanted me to show him my boobs and have me give him a hand job in the back seat of his car. He may or may not have mentioned something about finishing himself off on my breasts too."

I wait to see if she's joking, but sadly, I can tell what she's saying is the truth.

Then she looks at me, with the prettiest shade of blue eyes I've ever seen, and my heart almost stops. "For the record—guys are gross."

I chuckle at her surprising honesty. "Not denying that."

Men can be real creeps. I've seen the evening news. Sadly, there's just no arguing against her logic. Some of us are still good guys, but I don't say this to her. I just let her believe what she wants.

"I'm Alexei," I say, offering her my hand.

For a second, she just looks at my hand, and I don't think she's going to take it. But then finally, after deciding that she can trust me, at least for something as simple as a handshake, she places her small palm in mine and shakes my hand. She's freezing.

"I'm Ryleigh. Thanks for, um . . . saving me."

I haven't done anything yet. I wanted to punch that guy in the fucking jaw when I heard him propositioning her. Instead, I let him walk away unscathed. Lucky prick.

"Do you work here?" I lift my gaze to the neon sign blazing above our heads in the darkness. I scrub a hand over my face as I picture the petite woman standing before me scantily clad and serving drinks to a group of horny men with grabby hands and fat wallets.

She nods.

"You a stripper, then?" I ask.

Ryleigh makes an annoyed sound in her throat. "It's a topless bar. I'm not a stripper."

I knew as much, but part of me didn't want to admit I've been a customer at the place. It's not exactly a classy establishment. "But you serve drinks in your underwear."

"As I said, men are gross. Sadly, they also pay my bills."

I chuckle, again surprised by her. "I'm not denying it. And not that you asked for it, but in my point of view, men are visual creatures. And women are beautiful. We enjoy seeing them any chance we can get."

She merely rolls her eyes, clearly not buying my bullshit. "Listen, as nice as it is to freeze my lady balls off and stand out here talking to you, I need to find a way to get home."

"Where's your ride? I can wait with you." The words just stumbling out of my mouth before I can think about it.

"My car's in the shop, and my friend bailed on giving me a ride."

I nod, processing everything. Something also tells me she needs that three hundred bucks the guy was offering her. I take a deep breath, weighing my options. It's either go home alone to my $6 million penthouse and lie awake wondering if she's okay . . . or drive her home myself and convince her to just take the money I have in my wallet. It's not like I need it.

As tired as I was walking out of my dinner meeting with Slate, now I'm way too keyed up for sleep. It's then that I realize going home alone would be pointless.

"Is that what you needed the money for? Your car?"

Her inquisitive blue gaze meets mine, and for a second, I think she's going to deny that she needs the money. She'll probably try to save face by telling me I read the situation wrong, and she was never actually entertaining that scumbag's offer.

Instead, she surprises me for the third time in five minutes.

"No. Well, yes. But not tonight. My immediate concern is getting home and taking care of my roommate's baby."

"Baby?" I ask, lifting one eyebrow.

She nods, tucking a long strand of silky brown hair behind her ear. "My ex-roommate, actually. She, um, dropped off her baby a few days ago and left. I have no idea when she's coming back. I need to pick up diapers, more clothes, and baby formula. All of that stuff costs money." Ryleigh straightens, her posture stiffening, like she's revealed too much. "You know what, don't worry about it. I'll figure it out. I always do."

"Where's the baby now?" It's after midnight, after all. But no matter how late it is, I'm not letting her walk away just yet.

"My neighbor is babysitting her so I could work."

Something inside me believes Ryleigh's telling the truth. Even though the last thing I want to do tonight is deal with a sad woman who has what sounds like more drama than an episode of *Law & Order*, with an even more unusual twist of playing nanny for someone's baby, I find myself gesturing toward my car. My black Mercedes is parked right across the street.

"I'll take you."

She narrows her eyes. "I don't even know who you are. Why would I trust you?"

I don't point out that she was just considering getting into the car of a complete stranger. Or that she was considering doing unsavory activities with said stranger. I could tell her it's because I grew up with three sisters, and I have a big heart. I could tell her that I have six nieces and nephews, that I'm good with babies. I could even hand her my business card and tell her she could ruin me with one call to the media about how I tried to pick her up outside a nightclub. But I don't say any of those things. Instead, I find myself wanting her to trust me on instinct alone.

I finally settle on, "Because I'm offering to help you. No strings."

"No strings, as in I don't have to show you my boobs?"

I almost choke on the laugh that crawls up my chest. "Only if you want to, but remember . . . we men are visual creatures." I offer her my best playboy smirk, the one that usually makes women swoon, only to find it has no effect on Ryleigh.

S*trange.*

Maybe it's because she doesn't know who I

am, but she treats me differently than the women I usually meet, as if I'm a regular guy and not a famous millionaire sports star who easily melts women with simply a smile.

Ryleigh has no idea that I'm Alex Ivan, pro football player for the Chicago Hawks. She doesn't swoon and bat her eyelashes or try to impress me. In fact, she doesn't follow any of the normal protocols. Clearly, she's not a gold digger, because if she were, she could talk me out of way more than three hundred bucks. An even bigger part of me knows I could add several zeroes behind that figure, and she'd need every damn dime.

"Fine. I'll take the ride. But it's going to be a hard pass on the boobs."

"Whatever you want."

The truth is, she's gorgeous, and if she wanted to share her body with me, I'd jump at the fucking chance. But something about her no-nonsense demeanor tells me that's not going to happen, which is probably for the best. I don't have time to get tangled up in something right now, anyway. I have to focus on myself and my career now more than ever.

After another moment's hesitation, Ryleigh

looks back at the club one last time, and then to my car. I can see the moment she makes up her mind, letting out a soft sigh.

"Don't make me regret this," she mutters under her breath before she follows me to my car.

I hit the button on the key fob to start the engine, then unlock the doors. When we slide inside, I turn up the heat and direct the vents toward her.

"Thank you," she says, buckling her seat belt. "Nice car." Her gaze lingers on the sleek wood paneling, supple leather, and chrome fixtures.

"Thanks," I murmur, suddenly feeling a little sheepish about the opulence of my luxury sedan while she has to consider back-alley propositions just to feed her baby. No, not *her* baby, her ex-roommate's baby, which makes this entire situation even crazier. I shift into drive and pull out onto the road. "So, where to?"

"Oh, right." Ryleigh rattles off her address, and I wince.

I've only been to that area of the city once, and it was by accident because I was lost. It's not a safe or very nice area, and I hate to think about her walking around after dark alone, petite beauty that she is.

"So, your name, Alexei, is that . . ."

"Russian. My parents moved here when I was six." I also have no fucking clue why I told her my name is Alexei. Everyone calls me Alex. Everyone except for my mother and sisters.

"Do you remember much of it? Living in Russia? I've never been out of the United States. I've barely been out of the Midwest."

"A little. My parents tried to keep up the traditions for us. They were proud of their heritage. We spoke Russian at home, and every Friday, my mother would make a big traditional meal."

"What kinds of foods are in traditional Russian meals? Like borscht?"

I chuckle. "Borscht is disgusting." It's a beet soup that looks like a bowl of blood. "My favorites were the cabbage rolls and herb-and-meat-filled pies she would make."

"That sounds amazing. I haven't eaten a real home-cooked meal in a long time."

All this talk about food makes me wonder if she's hungry, if I should offer to stop and get something for her to eat. Then I decide against it because I don't want her to feel that I think she's a charity case. Plus, dinner together seems too personal, and I can't do personal right now. She's a big girl. She can feed herself.

The conversation I just had with my agent at dinner rings through my head. I need to keep my head down and stay focused on winning. Prove that I'm worth the huge contract that was just plopped into my lap. Period.

"What about you?" I ask. "Family in the area?"

She shakes her head, folding her hands in her lap. "I was an only child. Both of my parents have passed on."

"I'm sorry." *Shit*. Now I wish I'd never asked, because her story has gotten even more pitiful.

She shakes her head, still looking out the windshield. "It's okay."

We drive in silence for a few minutes, and when we get closer to her neighborhood, I spot a superstore that's all lit up on the corner, one of those twenty-four-hour places. I pull into the parking lot and park the car.

Ryleigh's gaze swings to mine, and I can sense the question on her parted lips.

I recall a piece of advice a coach gave me once

about how people would come out of the wood-work asking for money once I signed my first big contract. He recommended instead of giving out cash that I should give them what they need—you know, like paying an electric bill versus handing someone a hundred bucks.

"Why are you stopping here? My place is still a few blocks away." She gives me a curious look.

"Let's get the stuff you need." Plus, if she's lying about the baby, now would be the time to come clean.

She swallows and nods. "Thank you."

I grab a cart and we wander the store aisles, finally locating the baby section. She grabs a package of diapers, the smallest she can find, and places it in the cart. I know how quickly babies go through diapers. Those will only last her a couple of days, and I open my mouth to object. Then I decide I'm being a controlling asshole, and should let her do this her way. Next, we find baby formula, and Ryleigh selects a yellow tub of the stuff, groaning when she sees how expensive it is. Babies go through formula faster than diapers, and I know she needs a few of those tubs, but I stay focused on what she wants.

"What else do you need?" I ask, turning to face her.

Under the bright lights, I can see how truly beautiful she is for the first time. Her hair is the color of deep honey. It looked brown outside, but here in the light, shades of gold run through the soft waves. Her skin is like porcelain, soft and creamy, and her eyes are the most striking shade of blue, fringed in thick black lashes. *Stunning.*

As if she can sense me watching her, she chews on her lower lip and shakes her head. "I'm really not sure. I don't know the first thing about babies. She cries a lot, and I . . ."

"How old is she?"

"Two months."

I push the cart to the next aisle and find what I'm looking for. "Does she use one of these?" I ask, selecting a pacifier.

"I'm not sure. My ex-roommate left me with almost nothing. It's worth a shot."

I toss a couple of them into the cart and then grab a Boppy pillow. "What about one of these?"

Ryleigh's delicately arched eyebrows lift. "What the hell is it?"

I laugh again, amused by her honesty. "It's a special pillow. She can do tummy time. Sometimes the crying is due to gas bubbles. This could help."

"How do you know so much about babies?" Her eyes widen and lock onto mine.

I shrug, pushing the cart toward the checkout. "I have six nieces and nephews. I babysit them sometimes." *Whether I want to or not.* I smile, thinking about my sisters shoving one or more babies into my arms anytime we're at a family gathering.

We work together unloading the contents of the cart onto the conveyor belt. When the cart is empty, I pull out my gold card and hand it to the cashier.

Ryleigh stiffens. "You don't have to do that."

"I've got this, no worries."

She looks at me, and I can see the wheels spinning in her head. She wants to trust me, wants to think I'm being chivalrous and gallant, but she's wary because she's likely never had a white knight ride in and save her. I see her underlying distrust, and for some reason, I want to prove to her that tonight, her white knight is real.

Besides, I'm not letting her spend whatever tip money she made tonight on this. I'm sure she needs it for other things, like fixing her car or feeding herself, not for taking care of a baby unexpectedly dropped off on her doorstep. I still need to get to the bottom of that story, but I sense that now's not the time.

The cashier is watching our exchange with narrowed eyes. I smile and whisper to Ryleigh that she can pay me back if she likes, but it's really not necessary.

The cashier rings up the items we've purchased, and I accept the bags after sliding my credit card back into my wallet.

Once I have the bags loaded into the back seat of my car, we set off again. A few minutes later, we've arrived, and when I park on the street and step out of the car, I get angry.

Really. Fucking. Angry.

And my anger only intensifies with every step toward Ryleigh's apartment.

CHAPTER Two

Ryleigh

I have no idea how my night has spiraled so far out of control. Scratch that, not my night—my *life*.

My roommate, Andi, disappeared more than six months ago, leaving me high and dry with an unpaid rent bill. And then a few days ago, she appeared again out of nowhere, only this time with a baby, promising she'd pay me back and make everything right.

Stupidly, I believed her, let her in, and she stayed the night. But in the morning, she was gone, leaving little Ella behind with a note that simply said *I'm sorry*.

Alexei follows behind me, appraising everything. After I pay Mrs. Henderson and collect Ella, I unlock my front door and shoulder my way inside my darkened apartment. Alexei is right behind me.

I flip the lights on and wince. Based on this guy's car, his taste in clothing, and the way he whipped out his gold card like it was nothing to buy a stranger $70 worth of crap, he has money. Probably lots of it. I have almost none, barely enough to pay my rent and eat. And the decor shows it. Everything I own is secondhand. My brown couch sags in the middle, my dining chairs are mismatched, and my curtains are too short to fully cover the window.

I huff out an exhausted breath and set the baby carrier holding Ella onto the floor by the couch.

Alexei follows me around like a hulking lion of a man, his deep blue gaze seeing everything.

He's angry. That much is certain.

"It's freezing in here," he says, frowning.

His voice is irritated, but it still manages to rip through me like lightning. It's deep, rich, and sexy. It doesn't matter that I don't want to notice things like this about him; I just do. He's spellbindingly gorgeous with this commanding presence, and I hate that he's seeing me at my worst.

"I turn off the heat when I leave for the day." I cross the room and adjust the thermostat. But rather than the heat humming to life like I expect, nothing happens. I try again, cursing under my breath. "*Shit.*"

"What's wrong?"

I shake my head. No way I'm giving him the satisfaction of knowing I might not have paid the heating bill in time. I thought I had a few more days.

"Your heat doesn't work?" He crosses the room to inspect the thermostat. He switches the bags he's carrying to one hand while he fiddles with the settings, but nothing happens. The thing is ancient, and I'm not all that surprised.

Why didn't he just drop me off and leave? Why didn't I just take the bags out of his arms and thank him for the ride and the supplies? Why is he still here?

He still hasn't set the bags down yet, like he isn't sure where to place them, or maybe he doesn't want to touch anything here. Probably the latter. I wouldn't either if I were him.

I cross the room and reach for the bags, but he doesn't release them. He just gazes at me with those blue eyes, darkened to the color of midnight right now, eyes that see too much. His scent is intoxicating, and I can't help but breathe it in every time he's near, a faint combination of leather, spice, and mint that makes my knees weak. It's been way too long since I was with a man. About as long as it's been since I ate my last home-cooked meal, if my math is accurate.

As if on cue, Ella starts to whimper softly, squirming in her seat. The chilly temperature is probably bothering her.

I've been doing my best to hold it all together, not only for my sanity, but also for Ella's sake, but in this moment, I'm struck with sheer panic. *What the hell am I going to do now?*

Alexei doesn't give me a moment to even process the answer to that question. He simply struts over to the baby carrier and lifts it as though it weighs nothing at all. The damn thing hurts my arm every time I carry it.

"You guys are coming back to my place. We'll get this all sorted in the morning."

I cross the room to stand toe to toe with him and place my hands on my hips. "I'm sorry, but I don't know you from Adam. I'm not going home with a complete stranger."

"You don't have much of a choice. I'm not letting you and the baby stay here and freeze tonight. In case you didn't notice, it's below thirty outside, and it's not much warmer in here."

"Not *letting* me?" I sputter.

"That's right. Now, get your shit. It's way past her bedtime." His gaze flicks to Ella, whose whimper has turned into a full-on cry.

I sigh and reach for her, lifting her out and bouncing her in my arms. As I expected, it does nothing to calm her.

"Let me have her." He takes the baby from me and gently rubs small circles along her tiny back, having dropped the bags right on the floor. "When's the last time she's eaten?"

I check my phone for the time. It's almost one in the morning now. Mrs. Henderson said Ella had her last bottle at ten. "Almost three hours ago."

He nods. "She's due soon, but let's see if we can have her hold out until we get to my place. Then we'll put her down to sleep."

He continues patting her back, and when she lets out a huge burp, Alexei smiles. "There we go.

Was that the problem, princess?"

She stops crying briefly, blinking as she searches for the source of the deep voice.

Holding her carefully in one of his huge arms, he opens a package of pacifiers and washes one in the sink with my anti-bacterial soap, and then gives it to Ella. She immediately begins sucking away, and her renewed cries fade into soft hiccups.

I blink at him. "How do you know all this?"

He shrugs. "A gaggle of nieces and nephews, as I mentioned. I've been around babies a lot. You pick things up."

I've never spent much time around a baby, and these last few days have proved it. I have no idea what I'm doing with Ella, and I suddenly realize he's right. It is way past her bedtime, and it really is freezing here. I can't be selfish any longer. She's not mine, but I've been entrusted with her care. No matter how pissed I am at Andi right now, I need to do the right thing. For Ella.

"Fine. We'll come stay at your place for the night."

Alexei only nods, like he expected my response all along. "I'll get her car seat situated. You want to pack an overnight bag?" he asks, his voice softer. It still manages to tear straight through me.

"Yeah. It'll just take me a second."

He nods and heads outside into the cold, carrying both Ella, who is now happily sucking away at her pacifier in her carrier, as well as the bags of baby stuff we bought at the store.

Scrubbing one hand over my face, I muster the rest of the energy I have left and head into my bedroom to shove some things into a duffel bag. A change of clothes for both me and Ella, along with my toothbrush. In the kitchen, I toss in a couple of clean bottles, and a small package of baby wipes.

Then I fiddle with the thermostat one last time before giving up and heading out into the cold. Once I lock my front door, I rejoin Alexei in the car. It's warm and smells like him, and for some strange reason, that calms me more than it should.

"Ready?" he asks.

I turn to face him, taking in the dark scruffy hair dusted along his jaw, his broad shoulders, the firm line of his mouth. "Are you sure? You don't have to do this."

"It's fine, Ryleigh. It's just one night, right?"

I nod. "Do you have a roommate or a . . . a wife, or anything?"

"No roommate. Definitely no wife. It's just me. But there are two guest rooms, so you and . . . the baby can pick where you'd like to sleep."

"Her name's Ella."

"Ella," he repeats softly.

We're quiet on the ride to Alexei's place. It's on the other side of the city in an area known to be where the young, wealthy elite live. He pulls into an underground parking garage of a towering building, and has to show his credentials to a uniformed security guard who's working at the gate.

"Good evening, Mr. Ivan," the man says, his gaze wandering from Alexei to me, and then to the baby before widening in surprise.

"Night, Frank," Alexei says to the guy, then pulls the car ahead when the gate opens. He parks in a well-lit underground parking lot, and then we take the elevator up to the penthouse level.

I'm having a very Julia Roberts in *Pretty Woman* moment here. But despite what Alexei saw earlier, I'm not a prostitute, and he certainly won't be my knight in shining armor.

Suddenly, I'm struck by the need to correct him. "I wasn't going to do anything with that guy, you know."

He shrugs. "Not my business what you choose to do. I was merely trying to help you out of a situation I didn't think you wanted to be in."

I huff, pretty sure he doesn't believe me. "Well, for your information, I've never done anything like that. So if you think you're getting your dick sucked tonight or something, just because you bought us some diapers . . ."

Alexei holds up his hand. "Whoa. That's not why I brought you here. And no offense, but I can get my dick sucked anytime I want."

I have no idea what to make of *that* comment, like he's got a bevy of women at his beck and call. But then the elevator doors slide open, and for a second, I just stand there and stare.

I'm not sure what I was expecting, but his apartment is enormous. Polished marble floors and floor-to-ceiling windows that overlook the entire city dominate my view. There's a modern kitchen that's all stainless steel, white cabinets, and black granite, and a sunken living room with two huge, fluffy, cream-colored couches. The biggest flat-screen TV I've ever seen is mounted on one wall, and a hallway at the far end leads off to what I assume are the bedrooms.

"Come on in," he says.

I step off the elevator and follow him inside. Alexei sets the shopping bags on the counter while I free Ella from her car seat. Once she's in my arms, she begins crying again, and I let out a long exhale.

"May I?" he asks.

I pinch my lips together and hand Ella to him. I hate to admit defeat, but he does seem to know what he's doing more than I do.

She looks so tiny resting against his massive chest. It doesn't matter that the last thing I'm in the market for is a man, but seeing him with her does something to me. I think the technical term is ovary explosion. The way his big hands cradle her so carefully is so sweet that I nearly melt for this stranger who shouldn't affect me like this at all.

Needing to make myself useful, I grab one of her bottles from my purse and dig the tub of baby formula out of the shopping bag. "I'll feed her so we can go to bed and get out of your hair."

He shrugs. "It's no problem. I'm honestly more

of a night person."

I nod but continue making her bottle anyway. I doubt she'll last much longer. Over the past couple of days, I've learned that she likes to eat about every four hours. Everything has been trial and error since. Andi left me exactly zero instructions.

Alexei's deep voice interrupts my daydream. "There's bottled water in the pantry." He nods to the door at the end of the kitchen.

I go and grab a bottle of water and begin mixing up the formula.

"Are you hungry?" he asks. "You just got off work . . . I have pretzels, crackers, fruit, or I could make you a frozen pizza."

My stomach rumbles loudly at the mention of food. "That would be great, actually. Just something simple. Pretzels would be fine."

When the bottle is ready, Alexei reaches for it, uninterested in putting Ella down, it seems. I'm not sure why it surprises me that he'd like to feed her. He really is a natural with babies.

And even though I probably shouldn't, part of me just feels comfortable in his presence. It's unexpected, but I'm not complaining. "Would you mind if I took a shower? I actually feel kind of gross after I work."

"Not at all. Second doorway on the right. The towels are in the cabinet. Help yourself."

I nod, but then hesitate for a moment longer.

"I've got her, Ryleigh. You don't have to worry."

Smiling, I meet his eyes. I haven't had someone to help, someone to just be there for me in so long, that it makes my chest tighten. I have to turn away quickly because I'm afraid the emotional roller coaster I've been on since Andi left me with Ella will surface in front of Alexei, and I'm not sure I'm ready to be that vulnerable in front of this man.

"Thanks," I say finally, ducking out of the kitchen as I rush for the sanctuary of the bathroom and a shower that will wash my tears away quietly.

• • •

When I emerge from the bathroom, I hear Alexi cooing softly to the baby and singing her a lullaby in what I assume is Russian. She's cradled in his arms, her eyes sleepy as she looks up at him. The sight of her tiny fingers wrapped around his index finger almost brings me to my knees. Involuntarily, though, my mouth breaks into a smile as I listen for a moment longer. Then I clear my throat.

"Hey," he says, his lips turning up in a smirk. "Your shower okay?" His gaze wanders from mine down to my bare legs, and then back up.

My hair is damp, and I've changed into a pair of purple boxer shorts and an oversized T-shirt. I can feel my cheeks turn pink, but I nod and join him on the couch.

"That showerhead is seven-ways-to-Sunday amazing."

He chuckles. "Completely agree. That shower-head alone is worth double its price when you need to relax."

He places Ella so she's reclining on the couch, propped up by her new Boppy pillow and swaddled in her blanket like a little stuffed burrito.

"She took the whole bottle, and then I changed her. She should be ready for bed anytime."

"Thank you." I give her tiny pajama-covered foot a squeeze. It's only then that I notice the spread on the coffee table. A white platter contains a bunch of green grapes, sliced cheese, pretzels, and hummus.

"Wow. You didn't have to do all that, thank you." I help myself, popping a grape into my mouth.

"It wasn't any trouble."

Alexei watches while I eat, helping myself to a little bit of everything.

"This place is amazing. How long have you lived here?" I ask.

He considers my question, still watching me. "I moved to the city about three years ago."

"For work?"

He nods.

"What do you do?"

"I play for the Chicago Hawks."

It takes me a moment to process this. I'm not a sports person—not in the slightest. But I realize he's talking about the pro football team. "What position?"

"Linebacker."

I guess that explains why he's so huge. He's several inches over six feet tall, and at least a couple hundred pounds of solid muscle.

"Ah. It makes sense now." I pop another pretzel in my mouth, chewing slowly.

"What does?" he asks, lifting one dark brow curiously.

"That comment about getting a blow job whenever you want."

He shakes his head, his smirk fading. "I shouldn't have said that to you. It was very out of line for me."

I shrug. "What? I'm sure it's true. Women generally line up and drop to their knees for athletes, right? Like they're some special, secret aphrodisiac."

"But not you?" he asks, seeming amused by me.

I wrinkle my nose. "Sorry, no. Sports don't really do it for me. I'm more impressed you knew what a Boppy pillow is for."

Alexei chuckles, and I like the sound of it immediately. It's deep and rich, and uninhibited.

When I finish eating and look at Ella again, resting between us, her little eyelids have fallen closed. She's sound asleep.

"Can I ask whose baby this is?" he asks.

At first, I wondered if he might be skeptical, might think that she's mine. But given the fact that I have no idea what I'm doing with her, I think he knows I'm telling the truth. "My ex-roommate, Andi. She left her with me a couple of days ago. I've been trying to call her nonstop since, but her cell phone is turned off. I have no idea when she's coming back."

He nods, looking thoughtful. "Come on. Let's get you guys to bed."

I nod and rise to my feet, lifting Ella carefully so as not to wake her. Alexei carries the platter into the kitchen, wraps it in plastic, and sets it inside his refrigerator.

He leads us into a bedroom down the hall. There's a queen-size bed dressed in a fluffy white down comforter, and a Pack 'n Play set up in the corner.

Oh my God. The man comes complete with a Pack 'n Play. What planet am I living on?

"Thought this bedroom would be best for you. When I babysit my sister's littlest one, I put her down for a nap in here. Everything's clean, though. My housekeeper was just here and laundered all the bedding."

It's more than I could have hoped for. It's more than I have for Ella at my place.

"Thank you. This is perfect," I murmur, tears threatening to spill again.

Alexei is standing so close that I can feel the warmth radiating from his skin. I can feel his eyes on me, piercing me, as I bend over and carefully place Ella inside her bed for the night.

"If you need anything, my door's at the end of the hall. I'll keep it open. Just holler, okay?"

I nod, suddenly unable to form words at how sweet and kind this complete stranger has been to me tonight.

Alexei takes one last look at Ella before turning to face me. "Good night."

I watch the way his muscles bunch and move underneath his fitted long-sleeved T-shirt and jeans.

Everything about the past couple hours has been surreal. Too good to be true. I can't think about it without my heart clenching and belly tingling with nerves.

Once I turn out the light and climb into bed,

I realize how exhausted I am. I worked a double shift today, and all the muscles in my body are limp and tired. I relax into the feather pillows and close my eyes.

Lying alone in this room with the soft sounds of Ella breathing, I realize I have no idea what I'm doing, and no idea what I'll do tomorrow.

I have a lot to worry about—paying my rent and my heating bill, and taking care of Ella while trying to track down Andi. But right now, in this moment, I feel comforted and content, all thanks to a nice man who cared enough to help tonight.

As I look over toward the Pack 'n Play, though, I know that Ella is warm and fed. And that's enough to give me pause, because I don't know if I'll be able to say the same thing in a couple of days.

CHAPTER
Three

Alexei

I wake to the unfamiliar sounds of someone cooking in my kitchen—the sizzle of bacon in a pan, dishes clinking together. It's an unusual but not unwelcome sound. I've lived alone for the past eight years, ever since I graduated from college and went pro. Smiling, I swing my legs over the side of the bed and stand.

The morning erection tenting my boxers will need to be dealt with, but now isn't the time. Instead, I head into the bathroom and brush my teeth while I wait for it to deflate. Then I throw on some athletic shorts and a white T-shirt, and make my way into the kitchen.

Ryleigh's hair is piled on top of her head in a messy bun. Without the makeup she wore last night, she looks even younger. She's barefoot in my kitchen, singing the lyrics to some pop song that's constantly on the radio. She finishes cooking a skillet filled with scrambled eggs and turns off the gas burner.

"Morning," I say, my voice still raspy from sleep.

"Hi. Good morning," she chirps.

"You made breakfast?"

"There's bacon and coffee, and toast too. I figured being an athlete, you have a healthy appetite. And then I saw all the ingredients in your fridge. I hope you don't mind."

"Not at all. This is great."

I help myself to a mug and fill it with coffee. I usually don't bother making coffee at home, opting to pick some up on the way out instead. It's a rare treat to enjoy a morning like this at home.

"Where's Ella?" I ask.

"She woke up early, just before six. She's already napping again."

I nod, seeing that it's already eight. "I need to be at practice in an hour."

"I have to work later too. Will you drop us off on your way?"

"Uh . . . yeah, of course."

I don't like the thought of them going back to her apartment, especially since it doesn't have heat, but I hope to have that fixed shortly. I emailed my manager last night, gave him Ryleigh's address, and asked him to pay whatever she owed to the electric company so the heat could be turned back on.

I help myself to a plate piled with perfectly crisp bacon, eggs, and toast, then take a seat at the breakfast bar. "Aren't you going to eat?"

Ryleigh nods and takes a plate for herself. "Thank you. For everything. I mean, you could have just kept walking last night."

"I know, but that's not me." I run a hand through my hair.

"Why didn't you?"

Isn't that the million-dollar question. "The truth?" I say after swallowing a bite of bacon.

She nods, and brings a forkful of eggs to her lips.

"It's probably going to sound cheesy, but it seemed like you needed help. That guy seemed like a real fucking creep. Excuse my language, and my mom raised me better than to just walk by a woman in need."

A smile tugs up one side of her mouth. "You're quite the gentleman."

"Something like that." I don't want her to get the wrong idea about me. On the outside, I'm as gentlemanly as they come. But on the inside, I'm pretty much like every other red-blooded male. I like casual sex—a lot of it, most definitely watch too much porn, and I curse like a sailor when I'm with my boys. Minor details that will stay under lock and key because somehow I like her thinking that I'm just a gentleman.

"These are perfect, by the way." I take another bite of eggs. I swear they're the best eggs I've had in ages.

Ryleigh smiles as she watches me eat. "Glad you're enjoying them."

I want to hold her blue eyes captive, but don't want to unsettle her.

Ella lets out a cry from the bedroom, and Ryleigh hops down from the stool beside me.

I place my hand on her shoulder, stopping her. "Let me. You eat." I hate to think about the idea that this might be her only meal today, but it very well could be.

Ella is lying on her back, her tiny arms and legs flailing as she lets out frustrated cries. "Come here, little princess," I murmur softly as I lift her from the bedding.

I return to the kitchen and finish the rest of breakfast holding my fork in one hand and a soothed baby in the other.

Ryleigh shoots me curious glances whenever she thinks I'm not looking, and I'm not sure what to make of her expressions. I don't want her to think I'm overstepping some invisible "the help is nice now, but what happens tomorrow to Ella and me" line. But I do want Ryleigh to realize that there are good people in this world. Whether she wants to admit it or not, she's also one of the good people. She could have just as easily taken Ella to child protective services when her roommate abandoned her baby . . . but she didn't.

My heart beats over time when our hands brush

as she collects our plates. I'm not nervous, but I'm really, really aware of her. Her honey hair is starting to slip from her bun and for some strange reason I want to run my fingers through it.

After we clean up from breakfast, we pack up her and Ella's things and load them into my car. I have just enough time to drop them off at home and make it to the training facility. We ride in comfortable silence to her place. I linger at her front door as she unlocks it. I may have just met Ryleigh yesterday—this woman who stirs something inside me—but some part of me isn't ready to walk away.

"Thanks again, Alexei. I don't know how I could repay you for . . ."

I hold up one hand, stopping her. I don't want her to repay me. I meant what I'd said when I told her no strings. "It was really no trouble. If anything, I need to repay you for making those eggs this morning."

She smiles and takes Ella from me as she steps inside. "Have a good practice."

I nod, suddenly at a loss for words, and then it hits me. This is most likely the last time I'll see Ryleigh. We're strangers. She doesn't fit in my life, and I certainly don't belong in hers. And yet . . . I find myself reluctant to leave.

The realization that Coach will ride my ass if I'm even thirty seconds late makes me move quicker back to my car, but not before I turn and look back at this woman and the child who doesn't belong to her, and wonder what their future holds.

• • •

"Let's go! Where's the hustle, Ivan?" Coach yells from the edge of the field, and then blows his whistle.

I jog to the sidelines and take a deep drink of water. He's right. I'm distracted as fuck and playing like shit.

My teammates notice it, as do the coaching staff, and there's no excuse for it, other than Ryleigh. My mind is on her instead of practice.

I'm wondering if her heat got turned back on, if she'll be okay—and not just today. I find myself thinking about what happens next for her, which is crazy. That baby's not mine. I shouldn't even care. I've always taken great care to wrap my shit up every single time so I don't end up knocking up some girl and be in the same situation as her roommate. I've seen the huge responsibility of having a baby, and I'm in no fucking hurry to become a father.

But then why is my mind stuck on them both?

We finish practice, and I stomp off the turf toward the locker rooms.

"A word, Ivan!" Coach calls out from behind me.

Carrying my helmet, I jog back to where he waits.

"Something going on with you?"

I shake my head and try to move the knots that have settled between my shoulders. "Just didn't get enough sleep last night." *At least that much is true.* "I'll be ready for the game Sunday."

A vein throbs in his forehead as he runs one hand over the back of his neck. "You'd better be."

"Yes, sir." I nod and jog off, releasing a heavy exhale.

Frustrated, I move through my post-practice routine in silence, removing my pads and gear, stripping down, and showering under the warm spray. By the time I'm done toweling off, I don't feel any better, but I know what I need to do. I need to see Ryleigh. Need to see with my own eyes that she's fine, and then I'll move on, let them live their lives and I'll go back to living mine. She said she had to work today, so I decide that's where I'll go first.

I dress in jeans and a long-sleeved T-shirt. A few minutes later, I'm out the door and heading toward a certain topless bar . . . toward a certain woman who's constantly on my mind.

When I arrive, I park my car, making sure to lock it, and then head inside.

Blinking to allow my eyes to adjust to the dim interior, I approach the hostess station, already looking around for Ryleigh. I don't see her, but a blond hostess smiles at me and grabs a sticky menu as she steps out front to greet me. She's in a skin-tight black dress that's so short, I'm sure if she bent over, I'd see what color her panties are—if she's even wearing any panties in this "upscale" establishment.

"Hi, handsome. One for lunch?" she asks.

"Sure. Is Ryleigh working today?"

The blonde nods. "I'll seat you in her section. Right this way."

Frustration blooms inside my gut as I follow

her through the bar and toward the back where high-top tables and booths wait, mostly empty at this time of day. The walls are painted black, and red silk sheets hang from the ceiling, dividing off the space. Deep, seductive bass music thumps softly in the background.

After sitting in one side of the booth and accepting the menu, I still haven't spotted Ryleigh. The hostess flounces away, leaving me alone with my thoughts.

Part of me knows I shouldn't be here, but the other part of me won't be satisfied until I see her.

I thought I was prepared to see her again . . . until Ryleigh turns the corner and steps into my line of sight. What I wasn't prepared for is the heavily made-up version of Ryleigh wearing nothing but a tiny pair of glittery booty shorts. My heart begins beating like a snare drum inside my chest. Fuck.

She stops in her tracks when she sees me, her eyes widening almost comically large, and something inside me twists.

For a second I think she's going to run and hide, or at least try to cover herself. But then Ryleigh finds her composure, straightens her shoulders, and moves toward me.

As she struts closer, my mouth goes dry and my cock twitches in my pants. Her skin looks so soft and creamy, and her hair is flowing in loose waves down to her shoulders. Her breasts are perfect, not too large, but a nice handful that my palms ache to touch. Her nipples are tight and blush pink, and I want my mouth all over them. Now.

When she stops beside my table, I'm so hard and also so irritated that I've forgotten how to speak. The tiny shorts she's wearing are basically just a pair of panties, and there's some kind of delicate chain necklace thing around her hips. It's distracting as fuck.

"What can I get you?" she purrs, her voice low and seductive.

What the hell? Why is she acting like we've never met?

"I came to check on you," I say, my voice coming out too tight. "You okay?"

She bats her dark eyelashes. "Just peachy."

"Did your heat come back on?" I ask, straight to the point.

An annoyed look flashes across Ryleigh's face, and then she smiles at me again, only this time it doesn't reach her eyes, which have turned an icy shade of blue. "That's not for you to worry about, Alexei. I'm not a charity case, and despite what you witnessed last night, I'm a big girl and I can take care of myself. Now, would you like to order lunch or not?"

I fight the urge to roll my eyes at the tone of her voice. "Sure. Bring me a burger, please. Salad on the side. And a couple glasses of ice water."

"Right away, sir," Ryleigh says before strutting away, her shapely ass taunting me as she leaves.

I squeeze my eyes closed and huff out a sigh. It's a strange and unexpected reaction, but it makes me angry to see her here like this, knowing that any Tom, Dick, or Harry can walk in here and get an eyeful of her. I knew she worked here when we met, so I have no idea why it's suddenly giving me heartburn to see her in this environment. She's beautiful and almost naked, and it's pissing me right the fuck off.

Soon, she delivers two glasses of ice water, and I waste no time in drinking one of them in three big gulps. I'm usually dehydrated after such an intense workout and practice, but I'm pretty sure this is me attempting to quench my thirst for something else.

Without another word, Ryleigh turns to go again.

"Wait," I say, setting down the water as calmly as I can.

"Yes?" Her tone is clipped.

"How's Ella? Is she with your neighbor?"

Ryleigh nods. "She's fine, Alexei. Please stop worrying about us."

The way she says my name is too intimate, like we've known each other for years rather than less than twenty-four hours, like we're lovers and not virtual strangers. I like the sound of it way too much.

Ryleigh turns away to head back toward the kitchen, as if on a mission to get away from me as quickly as possible.

The next time she comes by my table, it's to deliver my food, which she does without a word. Normally, I'm ravenous after practice. Today, I barely manage to take a few bites before I push my plate away.

I hate that she has to work here where strange men look at her. I hate that her apartment is in a neighborhood that's so unsafe I don't even want to walk around there alone. I hate that her room-mate gave her more to worry about and take care of when she left Ella there with nothing.

Scrubbing my hands through my hair, I rise from my seat. I dig out my wallet and toss down a couple of bills, enough to cover my meal plus a $100 tip.

I need to leave before I do something stupid like beg her to quit.

And what would she do then, Alexei?

Come home with me again, my brain says, answering the unspoken question.

Not a good idea, and I know it. Yet, I still wish there was something I could do to fix this.

I find her lingering by the bar, where she's waiting as the bartender fills a drink order. I'd forgotten how much taller I am, but standing beside her emphasizes how petite she really is.

She spins to face me. "Your food come out okay?"

I nod and shove a piece of paper at her. "Here's my number. Please text me if you need anything. You or Ella. Okay?"

Ryleigh looks surprised, her big blue eyes peering up at mine as she accepts the scrap of paper. "Okay. But I won't need it."

Without a backward glance, I walk out with a hollow feeling inside my chest. A feeling of loss for something that was never really mine to lose.

CHAPTER
Four

Ryleigh

"**H**e's a freaking pro football player, Ry!" Desiree squeals, grabbing my upper arms as she jumps up and down.

"I know," I say, shrugging out of her grip to collect the money he left at the table, and count it. *Dear God . . .*

I'm still shaking from my exchange with Alexei. The last place I expected him to show up today was my work. Let's face it, I wasn't expecting him to show up anywhere in my world. I figured he'd run as fast as his athletic legs would carry him after he fulfilled his obligations from last night.

"Ry, I don't think you understand. That was *Alex Freaking Ivan*. And he asked to sit in *your* section," she says, still grinning at me like this is the best news she's ever heard in her entire life.

I'm a little surprised she recognized him, but then again, it's possible Desiree follows sports more than I do. Scratch that—if there are attractive men involved, of course she follows.

"Why don't you seem excited? He's one of the most talked-about players in the league right now. He got into some huge scuffle with a reporter at the end of the last season, and got suspended. He almost lost his contract. But then he signed a new and even better contract for thirty million dollars . . . as long as he can behave himself."

Thirty million dollars. I feel light-headed and have to press one hand to the sticky table and take several deep, slow breaths. I can't even imagine making thirty-thousand dollars right now.

I guess that explains why he throws money around like it's nothing. What does one single man do with that much money? And why does the *I can get my dick sucked anytime I want* discussion we had flicker in my mind in response to that answer? There's no way that Alexei pays for sex, not a chance. I quickly try to get that thought out of my head. Alexei's muscular body naked, his hips pumping . . .

S*top, Ry.*

"We've met once before," I say offhandedly to Desiree as I clear the rest of Alexei's uneaten lunch. I don't dare tell her that I stayed the night in his guest room last night. She'd probably drop dead from a heart attack on the spot.

"He's fucking hot. Tell me you're going to call him. Please, God, I'll call him if you don't and pretend I'm you!"

I roll my eyes and lift the tray. Not one to be easily dissuaded, Desiree follows me into the kitchen.

She's right. Alexei is hot. He's tall and muscular and gorgeous. But given the circumstances of how we met . . . the circumstances of my life right now? Yeah, the last thing I need is another complication, even a gorgeous and generous one.

"I don't know," I admit, and Desiree lets out a frustrated groan.

She pinches her lips together as she thinks this over. "Yeah, I guess it might not be good for him to be seen in public with someone who works at a topless bar. The media frenzy alone would be crazy."

She has an interesting point, and one I haven't considered. I'm trouble for a guy like him.

At first, I was horrified to have him see me here with my tits hanging out for God and everyone to see. But the way he looked at me? Like I was some lost puppy he needed to save? That felt like a punch to my gut. I won't be someone's pet project. Not ever. No fucking thank you.

So, I didn't give him the satisfaction of knowing he'd gotten to me. I just marched over to his table and treated him like any other customer. I put on my game face like I do for every other XY-chromosome who walks into the club, and pretended his look of pity didn't make me feel like the dirt on the bottom of his football cleats.

Yes, of course I'd love to meet a man as handsome and generous as Alexei someday, but not because I can't pay my rent and he wants to fix it for me. I want someone who wants me for *me*, who likes what I have to say, who thinks I'm funny and smart and beautiful. Not someone who sees a hot mess he needs to fix when he looks at me.

I don't need some knight in shining armor to come to my rescue, no matter how cute he is or how cute he looks holding Ella. It's really not fair to my ovaries to see a big, muscular man holding a baby. My mind wanders back to the way he sang to her in Russian. And yeah, how good he is with the baby only makes me feel more inadequate.

I'll prove to everyone, including Alexei, that I can take care of myself. And Ella.

Who am I kidding? I won't ever see Alexei again after the way I dismissed him a few moments ago like he was any other Joe in the club . . . like he didn't matter when he does.

• • •

By the time I get back home, it's raining. I worked the lunchtime shift and would have stayed through the evening shift too, but it was slow and my manager sent me home. Luckily, I made it to the auto-repair shop before they closed, and though I'm several hundred dollars poorer, at least I have my own car back and won't have to rely on ride-share services.

It never bothered me before, but coming back to the dumpy apartment complex I call home after having spent the night in Alexei's multi-million-dollar condo is a bit more depressing than usual. It doesn't help that the sky is gray and overcast, and dumping what feels like buckets of cold water down on me.

I stopped at the grocery store on the way and am finally arriving home. Carrying two heavy grocery bags, I trudge up the front steps. I'll pick up Ella from the neighbor's after I drop off the groceries inside. That's my last thought before the bottom of my paper bags give out, sending everything tumbling to the sopping-wet ground.

S*hit.*

Heaving out a sigh, I bend down and begin gathering the wet, muddy groceries, piling as much into my arms as I can hold. Shuffling to my door, I see there's a lockbox fixed around my doorknob. That wasn't there last night. I look up to find a yellow sheet of paper taped to the door, an eviction notice. Apparently, the locks have been changed, and I have to pay my back rent before I'll be allowed inside to retrieve my things. The landlord said I had another week.

F*ucking hell. Can this day get any worse?*

Before I can begin to process all of this, before I can start to cry, I hear the crunch of tires and a car stopping beside the curb. Somehow, I know without looking up who just pulled up behind me, which makes me want to cry even more. Tears burn the back of my eyelids and my nose tingles.

Alexei hops out into the rain wearing a hoodie and comes over to retrieve the canned goods, bananas, and various cartons and containers that I'm juggling. "You okay?" he asks in that same rich tone that I've come to both love and hate in a matter of two short days.

Why is he here? Why does he even care? Why does he always have to see me at my absolute worst? The universe hates me—that's the only explanation for this horrendous karma.

"I'm fine, Alexei. I told you that."

He cocks one eyebrow. "You don't look fine."

I'm sure I look like absolute hell with stringy wet hair plastered to my forehead, food scattered at my feet, and the eviction notice shining from my door like a gigantic beacon, announcing what a loser I am. Hit by another sudden wave of emotion, I pinch my lips together.

Alexei looks behind me, and I can see his brain registering the predicament I'm in right now.

"Come on. Let's get Ella. You're both coming with me."

My embarrassment may be through the roof, and there's no denying I need help. But somehow the anger and utter helplessness at my situation is projecting into my tone.

"I'm not your problem, or your little outreach project. You don't have to worry about me."

He nods. "Yeah, I know. Just like you didn't need to take in Ella when your roommate split. But it was the right thing to do, so you did it without a second thought. Come stay with me until things calm down for you and Ella."

In that moment, I realize that this is all I am to him. An obligation. His latest charity contribution. If he walked away now and the media got wind of it, it could irreparably tarnish his image. So, he has to do 'the right thing'.

"I don't know you, Alexei, and I can't just come live with you. I can't bring someone else's baby into your house and expect you to put up with everything that comes with taking care of a two-month-old, no matter how long this situation lasts." My voice is as strong as I can make it, but I swear even I can hear the lack of conviction in it.

"Ryleigh, this is no place for a baby. It's raining, and by the looks of it, you're homeless. All I'm asking is for you to let me be your Plan B."

I nod in defeat, the enormity of my situation

weighing me down so heavily that I'm not even sure which way is up. What I do know is that Alexei is here, and he wants to help us. I can't turn him away, even if I wanted to.

"Fine. Let me get Ella."

Alexei grabs the groceries from me to load into his car while I go to my neighbor's door to pay her for babysitting. After flipping up the cover on Ella's infant carrier to shield her from the rain, I hurry back to the car and place the carrier in the back seat. Alexei takes over, buckling her seat in place.

Still fuming mad about my life's turn of events, and horribly embarrassed, I climb inside his car. There's not one inch of my clothing that's dry, and I'm shivering but trying desperately to hide it, because I refuse to give in to it. I'm stronger than that . . . at least, I used to be.

Giving me a sense of déjà vu from the first night we met, Alexei cranks up the heat and directs all the vents toward me. Tears gather in my eyes at his ability to make me feel like I'm the most important thing in the world. I know I'm just something for him to fix, but it doesn't matter in that moment. Unable to say a word without tearing up, I stare blankly out the window and wonder if I'll ever get out of the messes I keep creating.

We arrive back at his place and get settled inside. I don't have anything to wear, and the only supplies I have for Ella are what were in her diaper bag. Alexei immediately leaves again, heading out into the rain to go get us what we need, putting me even further in his debt.

While he's gone, I strip out of my wet clothes and run a bath. Ella coos and flails her arms and legs while staring up at me, lying on a towel in the center of the bathroom while the tub fills. I realize that in four days of caring for her, I haven't given her a bath yet, and I suddenly feel like shit. I seriously have no idea what I'm doing. I strip her naked, throw her diaper in the trash, and cradle her carefully to my chest as I step into the warm water and ease us down.

Being skin to skin like this with her, hearing her happy little baby coos, is the first time I've really felt close to her.

"I won't let anything bad happen to you, sweet baby girl," I whisper, cupping warm water in handfuls to pour over her back.

I turn Ella and bend my knees so she can sit up against them while I lie back in the water. She enjoys her bath, kicking her little feet as I lather my hands with soap and wash her from head to toe.

"Hello? Ryleigh?" Alexei's voice calls from the hallway.

I didn't hear him come home.

"In the bathroom. We're taking a bath," I call back.

A moment of silence.

"Both of you?"

I chuckle. "Yeah."

"Okay. Let me know if you need a hand."

I roll my eyes, still smiling. "Thank you, but I'm pretty sure I've got this." I look at Ella and whisper in a silly voice, "We'll have to teach him that girls rule and boys drool, won't we, Ella?"

And with that, she laughs at the perfect moment, causing all the bad shit that's happened over the past four days to magically disappear from my mind as I laugh right along with her.

I finish bathing Ella and blow a few raspberries on her cute little tummy, and decide she looks even cuter with her skin pink from the warm water and with her fine blond hair wet and curly.

As I stare down it her, it suddenly hits me. *Damn.* With her in here with me, there's no way to wash myself, and no good way to get her out and dry her off without a second set of hands.

"Um, Alexei?" I call out.

"Yeah?" His voice is much closer than I expected, like he was waiting outside the bathroom door to come to our rescue if needed.

"Any chance you could come in here and help me get her out without looking?"

He lets out a deep chuckle. "Sure, but I wouldn't want to *drool* over anyone while I'm in there, being a boy and all."

Okay, I totally deserved that, but he had to know I was just joking with him. But was he trying to flirt with me with that comment? Nah . . . he was just mocking my comeback to him. That has to be it, right?

"Oh, so you heard the little heart-to-heart that I was having with Ella, huh?"

As I'm talking to him through the door, I frown down at myself. The bubbles have evaporated from our bathwater, and it's just miles of bare skin as far as the eye can see. More my skin than Ella's, of course. I sink my shoulders deeper in the water, like that will somehow magically cover my breasts from his view. I remind myself that he's seen these same breasts only hours earlier today.

"Come on in," I say in a resigned voice.

The door opens, and Alexei steps inside.

As he navigates around the pile of clothing I stripped out of, including a lacy black G-string, I swear I see a faint blush to his cheeks. Though it's dangerous even to fantasize about, I can't help but wonder if he likes what he sees.

When his eyes meet mine, I scold him. "I told you not to look!" Ella does little to shield my body from him. Traitor.

He smirks, looking even more handsome, if that's possible. "Nothing I haven't seen before."

Damn, why'd he have to bring that up when I'm already mortified? I tried to purposefully block that from my memory. I was just so mad he'd showed up at my place of work, barging in and acting like a possessive boyfriend when he doesn't really know me at all. If he did, he'd know how much I value my independence, how important it is for me to take care of myself. Ever since my parents passed, it's like I have a huge chip on my shoulder, and I need to prove to everyone how much I've got it together . . . even when I'm falling apart.

Alexei grabs a fluffy white towel from the cabinet and reaches for Ella as I hold her up. He wraps her securely so only her tiny face is peeking out, like he's done this exact thing a million times before.

My God, I don't know what's more adorable . . . Ella all bundled up in that warm towel with only her eyes showing, or the huge masculine man who's holding her and saying silly things to her as he tries to get her dried off. And I thought that smirk was sexy. A gorgeous man holding and caring for a baby is about the sexiest thing I've ever seen.

"I didn't think about the fact that I couldn't wash myself while I was holding her," I say, shifting beneath the water.

He nods, still grinning at me. God, that grin is lethal. It makes my belly tighten and flip, and my insides feel like mush.

"I figured. And she probably peed on you as soon as she hit the bathwater, maybe even a time or two."

"Ew. Gross. Okay, I'm definitely showering." I pull the drain on the tub with my big toe as Alexei turns his back, finally giving me some privacy.

"Take your time. I've got her."

I think those are the best six words I've ever heard. I also think if he were to say them to me again, I would melt in a puddle and flow right down the drain, along with the bathwater.

He leaves me alone to take a shower, and I find myself repeating those words in my head over and over.

When I emerge from the shower and trudge to the room I slept in last night, I find an array of shopping bags on the bed. I close the door and then peek inside each one.

There are three pairs of basic white cotton panties, a matching bra, warm fuzzy socks, T-shirts, a couple of pairs of boxers like the ones I like to sleep in, plus leggings and sweatshirts. Miraculously, everything is in my size. The man is nothing if not observant.

Still cold from standing out in the rain, I select the leggings and a soft gray sweatshirt, and get dressed, adding the socks at the end. I look down and wiggle my toes. Suddenly, I feel a bit like Julia Roberts in *Pretty Woman*.

It feels so strange to be standing here in his guest room, to be cared for in this way by a man

I hardly know. I know this is him being a generous person, but why do I feel like this could easily transform from the friend zone to something more sinful?

I brush my hair with the comb from my purse, and then head out to the living room to find Alexei and Ella on the couch. He's already diapered her, and is cutting the tags off a pink-yellow-and-white-striped pajama onesie with little ducks on the feet.

Oh my God, he's combed her hair. I almost orgasm on the spot. It's parted on the side and combed neatly into place. My ovaries could compete on one of those dancing-competition shows with how active they've been today.

"This is all way too much, Alexei," I say, joining him in the living room.

"It's nothing, Ryleigh. I promise. Besides, she's a girl and needs to be worshipped like all girls do."

My throat feels tight when I swallow. Why am I reading between the lines with what he just told me? A couple hundred dollars in clothes and diapers and formula is nothing to him. But to us? It's everything.

Suddenly, I want to show him my gratitude, want to kiss him senseless and thank him in every single way I know how. Maybe even invent a few new ones. Instead, I rise to my feet and head into the kitchen. I need to put some distance between us before I do something I'll regret.

"I know how to cook more than breakfast food," I tell him. "Should I find something to make us for dinner?"

"Sure. That'd be great," he says. "I think I have stuff for pasta or stir fry. There's chicken and ground bison, and I'm not sure what else."

Bison? Um . . . no thanks.

I open his fridge, and it's like a food utopia. It's all completely organized with glass containers filled with cooked rice, grilled chicken breasts, roasted sweet potatoes, and greens, and cartons of fresh berries. There are at least half a dozen avocados, and even individual jars of overnight oats with slivered almonds.

"Holy hell. This is amazing."

Alexei chuckles. "I have to eat well during the season. And I go through a lot of food. My housekeeper is also my food shopper and preparer since cooking isn't really my thing."

"I can see that." My fridge is sad in comparison. Bottled mustard and old pickles, along with a half-empty bottle of white wine.

Relieved that there's at least something I can do to make myself useful, I select the ingredients for chicken marsala. There's thawed chicken breasts and two cartons of mushrooms, along with the shallots and whole garlic cloves I spotted on the counter earlier. My mouth is practically watering already. Anything is better than instant noodles, but this is heaven.

Something inside me wants to impress him. I have zero to offer this man in return for his kindness, and he's already done so much for Ella and me. I'll show him my appreciation through his stomach—instead of in his bed like I wanted to do a few moments ago. I won't sleep with him.

So I begin the food preparations, wanting to surprise him with how well I can cook. I have the chicken coated in flour and cooking in a sauté pan when he strolls into the kitchen carrying Ella.

"We could open a bottle of wine," he says when he sees the direction I'm headed.

I fill a pot with water and turn on the gas burner. Even his stove is incredible—a six-burner gas range that looks like it belongs in a commercial kitchen.

"I didn't think you'd drink, what with being Mr. Healthy and all." I smile at him. It appears my bath and the clean clothes have done wonders for my spirits.

"I can have a glass. But if you don't want one . . ."

"I'd love a glass," I say.

While I sauté the mushrooms, shallots, and minced garlic in another pan, Alexei uncorks a bottle of chilled white wine. He pours two glasses and sets mine on the counter beside me.

I pick up the fine stemware and turn to face him. "Cheers," I murmur.

He clinks his glass to mine, one hand still holding Ella. "Cheers."

His gaze lingers on mine as I bring the glass to my lips and take a sip. The temperature in the kitchen soars about six thousand degrees, and it has nothing to do with the heat from the stove or the wine. His eyes on me are intoxicating.

As Alexei turns to prepare Ella's evening bottle, I wonder how I'll possibly keep my hands to myself when this gorgeous man is strutting around looking like sex on a stick, all while doing nothing more than holding a baby who doesn't belong to him. I can't stop thinking about it. Every time he does something with Ella, my ovaries think for me.

I'm totally screwed.

CHAPTER *Five*

Ryleigh

These last few nights have been nice, but apparently Alexei has gone and lost his freaking mind.

When he told me this morning he's flying to California later today for an away game, I started packing, assuming I'd obviously have to find another place to go. He disagreed, and now we've been arguing about this for the past thirty minutes.

He's insane, absolutely insane. And now he's staring at me with that sexy, determined expression, his fists clenched at his sides. If it's a fight he wants, it's a fight he's going to get. *Bring it, buddy.*

I square my shoulders and summon the most

commanding tone I can muster. "I can't stay here while you're gone."

He swallows, his Adam's apple bobbing in the most distracting way. "Of course you can. I offered. You'll accept. It's a done deal." His eyes are playful, but his stance says he means business.

Well, two can play at that game, dude. I'm not intimidated by the fact he's a professional athlete. I can and will hold my own.

"It's not a *done deal*. I won't stay here, Alexei. End of story. You've already been too generous, too kind. I won't take advantage of you like that. I'm practically a stranger, and you can't possibly trust me alone in your home."

I mean, seriously. The dinner, the bath, the heavenly comfortable bed—everything has been great, but I've known all along it's a very temporary solution to my problem.

He smirks, somehow going from angry to amused in about 3.5 seconds. "Oh yeah? And why not? Are you going to make chicken parmesan? Take a bath in my tub? Use all the towels? Do a load of laundry? Be my guest."

I roll my eyes. "Have you been hit in the head too many times on the field? No, you big bossy man. You can't invite a random woman to live here while you're away. I could . . ." I look around, searching. "Steal your TV, or . . ." *Jeez, I would make the worst criminal ever.* "I could go through your bank statements and tax returns, start a fake identity with your social security number. Maybe commit a murder in your bedroom."

His eyes widen as he considers my words.

There. Take that, you big oaf!

Then Alexei chuckles and shakes his head. "You're not going to do any of that." He stalks closer to where I'm standing until we're just a foot apart. Then he places his big calloused palms on my upper arms and gives them a light squeeze. I've wondered since the day I met him what his touch would feel like. It's the first time he's touched me so intimately, and I know he's not doing it to be sensuous, he's only doing it to convey his trust in me, but the effect is the same. My skin tingles pleasantly and my breath hitches in my throat. Desiree's words about Alex Ivan being one of the world's most sought-after men ring through my head.

His voice drops lower, his anger gone. "I trust you, okay? Is that so crazy?"

His hands fall away and I pull in a deep breath,

his words both calming and alarming me. We hardly know each other, but there's this *thing* happening between us—undeniable as it is.

"It's crazy, yes. You and I both know it's insane."

Alexei mulls this over, his perfectly straight white teeth biting into his bottom lip as he does. "I didn't want to say this, I wanted you to stay because you wanted to, but . . ."

I rock back on my heels, waiting for whatever bomb he's about to drop on me.

"We both know this is what's best for Ella. Moving her back and forth, disrupting her schedule like that, it's not good for her. This is what's best for *her*, and since I want you guys here . . . Stay. Please."

Ugh, low blow. I hate when he reminds me that I'm not capable of taking care of her on my own, even if those aren't the words he used.

I straighten my spine. "Fine. We'll stay."

His full mouth breaks into a happy grin. "Good. That was easy. Now, let's talk about your place of employment . . ."

I shake my head, frowning at him. "Don't say

a word, buddy." He's been driving me to work and my old neighbor watches Ella until I get off and he comes back to pick us up. I'm not sure what the plan is when he's gone, but my job is one thing he doesn't get to dictate.

Alexei only chuckles, but I can tell he was serious, and this is a topic of conversation we'll be discussing in the future. God, this man. He's equal parts gorgeous and infuriating.

He may have won this round, but I have no intention of giving in so easily.

CHAPTER
Six

Alexei

've just boarded a plane to California, but all I can think about is the woman and baby I'm leaving behind.

It took quite a bit of convincing to get Ryleigh to stay at my place while I'm away this weekend. I almost thought I'd have to threaten to tie her to a chair, but in the end, she finally agreed. It should be strange, I've known her only a handful of days, and yet I trust her completely in my personal space.

My agent, Slate, thinks I'm insane, but he hasn't met Ryleigh. She's the furthest thing from a gold digger you could find. I've had to fight with her every step of the way to get her to let me help.

Even the smallest things are difficult with her. She's insisted on cooking for me as a way to earn her keep, which has been fine with me. I hate cooking, but I need to eat so often, it's a necessary evil. Ryleigh seems to enjoy it. She's made herself at home in my kitchen, and loves coming up with new dishes for me to try. The homemade fettucine alfredo she made last night was almost as good as sex.

Scratch that.

It was amazing, but yeah, nothing is as good as sex. Living with a gorgeous woman I've seen naked twice has fucked with my brain. Now I have sex on the brain like a horny teenager. *Fantastic.*

I'm way overdue for some action, but there's no way I can hook up with some random woman while Ryleigh and Ella are staying with me. At this point, I'm pretty sure the only woman I could get it up for would be Ryleigh.

How does this woman I barely know own me already?

My mind keeps remembering those tight-ass shorts she had on at the club and those gorgeous tits. Jesus, those tits and everything that's below them have haunted my dreams. I've dreamt about her every night. Touching her. Kissing her. Rolling her nipples under my thumbs.

Unfortunately, she hasn't shown the least bit of interest. Actually, that's not entirely true. After dinner during her second night there, she lingered in the kitchen, standing close, her pretty blue eyes locked on mine, and for a second, I got the feeling that she wanted me to kiss her—or that she wanted to kiss me. Fuck, I wouldn't have complained either way.

But there was no way I was going to make things awkward and freak her out. For all I knew, she'd panic and hightail it out of there. The thought of her and Ella out there somewhere fending for themselves wasn't a chance I was willing to take, especially not in the middle of winter in Chicago.

So instead, I busied myself with cleaning the kitchen. Ryleigh left to lay Ella down, and when she came back and washed bottles beside me at the kitchen sink, all the tension from earlier was gone. We shared another glass of wine and talked about our favorite movies before parting ways to head off to bed—in separate bedrooms. It didn't stop me from jacking off that night while thinking of how she looked in the bathtub, but at least I didn't do something stupid like make a move on her.

She gets hit on all day every day at her job, and I'm not about to be like one of those Neanderthals and expect her to share her body with me just because I'm helping her. If and when she decides to share that delicious body of hers with me, it will be because she's as desperate as I am to explore what could happen between us, not because she feels like she has to share my bed for a warm place to stay.

"You ready for the big game, Ivan?" my friend Doug asks, clapping one hand on my shoulder as he passes me in the aisle to take the row behind me. The plane is big enough that each player has his own row, which is helpful when you stuff sixty-five football players onto a plane together.

"Born ready, baby," I quip.

The truth is, the game is the furthest thing from my mind, and I hope I can get through it without letting my team down.

I pull out my phone to text Ryleigh one last time before we need to switch over to airplane mode.

```
Hey, Ry—you guys okay? We're
about to take off.
```

A second later, my phone pings, and my mouth twitches in a smile.

> We'll be fine, Alexei. Go win that game. For me and Ella. :)

I chuckle and tap out a reply.

> You going to watch me on TV?

I watch as the last of the players and staff board the plane and wait for her to reply.

> Oh! I never thought of that. Yeah, totally! What time's the game? What's your number again so I know who to look for on the field?

This makes me laugh harder. I've never dated a woman who wasn't obsessed with football, obsessed with what I did for a living or the idea of being a player's girlfriend or wife. Ryleigh literally has zero interest, and I find that refreshing.

I fill her in on the time and tell her which channel she'll find the game on, as well as the number on my jersey.

See you Sunday night.

Her reply comes almost instantly.

Looking forward to it.

Two nights. Two nights away from Ryleigh and little Ella, and it feels like a fucking eternity.

• • •

I have no idea what the hell is happening to my life. I only know that all my concentration, all my focus, has been replaced with constant worry and concern for a certain woman and baby who are currently staying in my home.

My team squeaked out a win, but only barely, and I can tell Coach Royce isn't at all pleased with my performance on the field. But fuck it. We won. It's over. He's just going to have to deal with it for now.

On our flight back to Chicago, I lean my head back against the seat with my eyes closed, pretending to be asleep so I don't have to endure any questions about what the fuck happened out there. During the last forty-eight hours, I became someone I barely recognized. I was like a needy teenage boyfriend, texting Ryleigh constantly, checking on them, and honestly just missing having them near. Even little Ella.

I almost had a panic attack and flew back when Ryleigh couldn't figure out how to arm the alarm system, even though there was no way anyone was even getting up to the apartment without my passcode. Basically, I was being a ridiculous man-baby about all of this, and I have no freaking idea why.

While I was halfway across the country wishing I was back in Chi-town, Ryleigh spent her time being productive, trying to track down Ella's mom, and even filed a missing person's report with the police, although she hasn't gotten anywhere with her search. I bet she wasn't checking her phone constantly and about to go all full-blown meltdown while worrying about me.

Jesus, I need to get my head and possibly my balls checked. Hell, maybe even a check to see if a vagina is growing in place of my manhood. Nothing would surprise me at this point.

When my ears pop from the change in pressure,

I open my eyes, happy we'll be landing soon. Forty minutes later, I pull into the parking garage of my building. I can't get to the elevator fast enough, and jab the button three times in my rush to get upstairs.

It's late, almost ten here, and I find Ryleigh curled on the couch with a glass of white wine in her hand. Her legs are covered by a white fur throw, and the TV is on mute. Ella is nowhere to be seen, in her Pack 'n Play, I'm sure.

"Hi," I say.

"Hey." Ryleigh grins when she sees me and starts to get up.

"Don't move. You look comfortable," I say, joining her on the other end of the couch. I lift her bare feet and place them in my lap. I need to touch her right now. I know I shouldn't, but tonight I'm indulging. I'm too weak not to have my hands on her after the weekend away from her.

"I am. She wore me out." Ryleigh lets out a yawn as I rub small circles into the arch of her foot. "Mmm . . . that feels nice," she says, closing her eyes.

She looks so pretty like this, so soft and domestic. There's something I like about finding her here waiting for me, all relaxed and sleepy.

"Did you watch the game?" I ask.

Ryleigh's eyes open and latch onto mine. "You were amazing, Alexei. I've never been more interested in watching a football game in my entire life."

I chuckle. "I played like shit, but thanks."

"No way. I thought it was amazing. You were so confident and aggressive. It was . . . never mind."

"It was what?" Curiosity makes my mouth quirk up.

"It was hot," she says quietly, her gaze dips from mine to my mouth and then back up.

"Glad you enjoyed it," I say, my voice suddenly tight as my hands stop their gentle caresses while we stare at each other.

She nods. "I only have one complaint."

"What was that?" I move to the other foot to give it the same treatment now that it seems our moment has passed. I've never dared to touch her this freely, but somehow it just feels right. And she's letting me, so there's no fucking way I'm stopping now.

"I wish they had more coverage of you."

This makes me laugh. Coming from her it sounds adorable and slightly awkward, but I don't care, I feel ten feet tall. "I'm a linebacker, not the quarterback. They get the most airtime." Truth be told, I'm lucky to make it on a few clips here and there.

She swallows, watching my hands work on her delicate foot. "Well, I much preferred watching you."

It's in that moment that I wonder if she feels the same way I do. Does she feel this thing between us? The force field of chemistry zapping around us is intense. It makes me wonder if this could be something real, and not just something physical—though I know that the physical could be really fucking amazing too.

I sit up and move closer. Ryleigh straightens too. I take the glass of wine from her hands and set it on the coffee table.

"Is it crazy if I say that I missed you?" I murmur, my mouth just inches from hers.

Her eyes are so blue, so wide and clear. They're mesmerizing.

She wets her lips with the tip of her tongue. "I . . . I missed you too. I mean, mostly I just missed having backup with the baby, if I'm being completely honest, but the other part of me missed you."

I laugh and place my hand on her neck, my fingers turning her head toward me. "Come here."

When I draw her close, Ryleigh tilts her mouth up, and I place one slow, sweet kiss against her parted, damp, wine-flavored lips. Heat races down my spine, and my cock hardens instantly. One slow kiss becomes two and then three, and when my tongue slips between her lips, Ryleigh reciprocates, deepening the kiss and making me groan.

I thread my fingers through her silky hair and kiss her pretty, pouty mouth like my life depends on it. She makes a small, need-filled sound that makes my cock ache.

Breaking away from her lips for a second, I pull her onto my lap. Ryleigh parts her knees on either side of my thighs, bringing her pussy in line with my now fully erect dick.

I grunt at the surprise contact. It feels so fucking good.

"Oh, hi there," she says, smiling at me.

"Hi."

She places one hand on my cheek and leans in for another kiss, giving her hips an experimental roll.

Fuck.

She's torturing me. Scientific fact: I will die if I don't get inside her in the next four seconds.

I settle my hands on her ass and tug her even closer. "You are so fucking sexy, baby."

When I tug at her T-shirt, Ryleigh raises her arms, letting me pull it off over her head. She's bare beneath, and I waste no time filling my hands with those gorgeous tits.

"Alexei . . ." She groans my name when my thumbs find her nipples and tease.

Her back arches and my mouth moves from her neck to her chest, where I suck and flick the firm peaks with my tongue until she's writhing in my lap.

I think my head's going to explode. Correction: both heads.

"Baby," I pant. "I don't want to pressure you. Don't want to go further than you're comfortable with . . ."

Ryleigh nods like she agrees, but she doesn't tell me how far she wants this to go. Instead, she slips her hands under my shirt and presses both small palms flat against my abs, her face lighting up in happiness at the firm muscles she finds there.

Soon, I've stripped her of her leggings, leaving her in only a pair of those damn white cotton panties I bought her. Her wavy hair drifts over her shoulders, and she looks like a goddess perched above me, grinding against my dick.

I'm still wearing my jeans, but Ryleigh's rid me of my shirt, and she can't seem to stop rubbing her palms all over my chest and abs. I'm not ashamed to say that I'm loving her hands all over me, no matter where they are. It feels really fucking good, and even though I want more, a lot more, I'm happy to let her set the pace.

Then she reaches between us and unbuttons my jeans, and my heart rate triples.

"Fuck, are you sure about this?" I kiss her throat as her hands work inside my boxer briefs. I can't stop praising her, can't stop kissing her, can't stop wanting her. I never want this to end, but I need to hear her say that she wants this too.

She stills unexpectedly. "Wait."

I pull back, terrified she's come to her senses and is going to put the brakes on this whole thing. "What is it?" Blood pounds through my veins.

Her nose scrunches up. "You didn't, like, sleep with a whole bunch of groupies while you were gone, did you?"

I smooth my thumb over the worry lines in her forehead. I can't blame her for being worried. The shit some of my teammates do isn't exactly a state secret. "No. I haven't slept with anyone in months."

This makes Ryleigh smile.

"Why are you worried? You didn't have a whole bunch of dudes over while I was gone, did you?" I'm kidding, but I can't help but tease her a little. At the same time, the thought of it makes my blood heat.

She swats my arm. "I haven't been with anyone in almost a year."

That news is surprising. She's beautiful, and so sweet. "In that case, I think you deserve the deluxe treatment." I smirk.

"Hmm." She grins. "And what does the *deluxe treatment* involve?"

"Come here." I stand, lift her in my arms, and

carry her to my bedroom, where I place her on the bed. Then I tug her closer and press her thighs apart as I lower myself into the space between her legs.

"Alexei . . ." She begins to protest, and then I draw her damp little panties down her legs. And when my tongue meets her silken wet core, her protests fade into cries of pleasure.

"Lie back and enjoy, baby. I intend to taste every inch of you tonight."

I lick and suck at her tender flesh, holding her hips still with my hands. She tastes so good. All sweet, feminine arousal, and knowing it's for me makes me impossibly harder.

Within minutes, Ryleigh's cries change into something more primal. She's so damn close. Her pants and heavy breaths are about to make me come in my damn jeans like a teenager.

I push one finger inside her tight heat and groan at how good she feels. Ryleigh cries out, lifting her hips to rock in time to my movements. Another lazy circle of my tongue and she comes, her body clenching around my finger as she cries out, panting my name.

It's the best fucking sound in the entire world.

A few moments later, I join her on the bed, kissing and nibbling her inner thighs as I move up her body to lie beside her.

Her hazy eyes blink open and find mine. "Wow. I think I'm a huge fan of the deluxe treatment," she says, her voice breathy.

I can't help the chuckle that tumbles from my lips. Her honesty always gets me. Most girls I meet are only after my status, and are thrilled that I'm giving them the time of day, most likely with the hope that they'll become a permanent fixture in my life. Ryleigh doesn't care about that, and she's fought me every step of the way up to this point.

When her warm palm cups me through my boxers, my smile fades. I'm trying to rein in the desire I have for this woman, but she's making it more difficult than I thought . . . that and the amount of time since I've been laid are at war with the gentlemanly pedestal Ryleigh has placed me on.

"Can I touch you?" she asks.

"Fuck yes."

Ryleigh plants a kiss to my chest on her way down, stopping to tickle my ab muscles with her tongue until she's eye to eye with her prize.

I tug my boxers and jeans down in one swift movement and chuck them over the side of the bed. Ryleigh's eyes widen as she takes me in.

"Oh, Alexei." She groans, wrapping her delicate fist around my swollen shaft and giving it a firm stroke.

O*h God.*

I release a guttural noise, and my eyes fall closed. I've wanted her hands on me since I first met her, and this is almost too much. Sensation overload takes over all rational thought.

"Yes, baby. Stroke me, please." I'm not above begging, because her hand beats my hand every day of the week.

But Ryleigh has other ideas. She lowers herself between my legs, her back arching as she brings her mouth to me. The curve of her bare ass is distracting, and my gaze moves between that enticing view to the slow, wet kiss she's currently treating the head of my cock to that feels so damn good.

"Oh, fuck yes." I growl when she swallows my whole length all the way to the back of her throat.

So good.

It's so, *so* good.

Then she adds a hand, twisting her palm as it slides up my firm shaft, and I know I'm going to come way too soon and embarrass myself. But in this moment, I couldn't give two fucks.

Pushing my hips up off the bed, I can't help but fuck her mouth.

"Too good. Fuck, Ryleigh. *Shit.* Yes, baby."

Her eyes are closed in concentration, and her dark eyelashes rest against her high cheekbones. She's beautiful. A few more wet strokes and I come, erupting into her mouth in a series of hot jets that make me see stars.

Ryleigh, always surprising me, swallows every drop, making needy little sounds in the back of her throat.

F*uck.*

This girl.

When she's through, she crawls back up my body and presses a soft kiss to my neck.

"That was fucking incredible," I croak, my voice tight as I try to slow down my breathing.

She giggles. "Glad you liked it."

I pull her closer and kiss her on the lips, threading my fingers through her hair. "Liked it? Baby, I fucking loved it."

As if on cue, Ella lets out a cry from the next room, and Ryleigh stiffens.

"Relax. I've got her." I rise from the bed and tug on my boxers.

"She's hungry. There's a bottle already in the fridge."

I lean down and press a kiss to Ryleigh's temple before shuffling out of the room, feeling like the luckiest fucking man in the world.

CHAPTER

Seven

Ryleigh

I wake up to the sound of Ella crying, which is nothing new. But when I blink my eyes open, it takes me a few moments to adjust to my surroundings.

Instead of the white walls and fluffy white duvet I've become used to the past few nights in the guest room, I see navy blue walls and dark gray bedding. And I'm surrounded by the best scent in the entire world—Alexei's masculine scent of leather and spice.

M*mm.*

I fell asleep in his bed last night, in his arms, it seems . . . and somehow it just feels right. A smile graces my lips as I sit up, ready to swing my legs over the side of the bed to go take care of Ella, but firm hands circle my waist and tug me back to bed. Or, more specifically, toward a hard-muscled chest. Heat zips down my spine at the memory of what we did last night.

"Don't go. Not yet," Alexei says in his deep, sexy voice, making my toes curl. He nips at my neck and sends shivers down my spine.

I don't want to leave the warmth of his muscular chest, but a whimpering baby is a powerful pull. "She's hungry. I've got her this time."

"You sure?" he asks.

"Positive." I pat one hand against his firm abs, and this time I succeed in escaping his arms.

"Okay," he says sleepily as he rolls over to doze back off.

I tiptoe from the room, grab my pajamas, and quickly dress before I reach Ella. She smiles when she sees me, and my heart melts at the sight of her gummy baby smile.

"Hi, pretty girl," I say as I lift her out.

We head to the kitchen and I make her a bottle. As I sit on the couch and begin feeding her, I stroke her hair and watch her drink. Her bright blue eyes latch onto mine as she takes greedy pulls from the bottle. For some reason, sitting here with her, both of us still dressed in our pajamas, it makes me feel oddly emotional.

"I'm going to find your mom. I promise."

Ella blinks up at me, and I lift her to my face, pressing a soft kiss against her forehead. I hold her tiny body close to mine as she makes progress on the bottle.

It strikes me again what a mess my life is. I'm sitting here with a baby, part of me still reeling about that, the other part of me feeling like I'm on cloud nine because of how sweet and sexy Alexei is, and how good he is with his tongue—but the truth is, things are far from okay. I was evicted from my apartment, Andi is still dodging my calls, I have to work today, and I'm worried about how Alexei will act when I tell him I have to go to work.

He strolls out of the bedroom a short time later, freshly showered, and dressed in jeans and a T-shirt. His long feet are bare, and his hair is still damp. He looks good enough to eat.

Focus, Ryleigh.

He starts a pot of coffee and then joins us in

the living room, leaning down to touch Ella's foot. "Good morning, princess," he coos.

I lift Ella to my shoulder and pat her back to burp her. Like the good little baby she is, she makes a loud burping sound almost instantly, and Alexei chuckles. I take a deep breath, hoping on the fact that he's in a good mood. "I'll need a ride to pick up my car today," I say, testing the waters.

"Sure. We can go after breakfast, if you like."

W*ow. That was easier than I thought.*

"And, um, I'll need to drop off Ella with my neighbor so I can go to work."

"You have to work today?" he asks, his voice tight.

"Yes. From noon to six." I hold my breath, waiting for him to make some comment forbidding me from going. Ella lets out one more small burp, and I place her on her special pillow on the couch beside me.

Alexei heads into the kitchen and pours himself a cup of coffee. "I can watch her. There's no need to get a babysitter."

I go back to folding the pile of freshly washed baby blankets, but there's shock written all over my face. He surprises me at almost every turn. "You would do that?"

"Sure," he says offhandedly. "Why not?"

"You don't have work today?"

"When we win a game, there's no practice the following day. It's a little perk they give us. I'm supposed to go in for an hour later for a team meeting, and we watch some of the highlight reel from the game. That's it."

"But what about Ella?"

He shrugs, heading back to the living room with his coffee mug in hand. "I can take her with me. It's no big deal."

No big deal? "What will your teammates say?"

"I don't give a fuck what they say."

I smirk to myself. They'll probably think she's his.

Why does the idea of that make my lips curl up in a smile?

I realize if people saw all three of us out together, they would think we were Ella's parents, and I can't help but wonder what that would be like. To be part of a couple, part of a family again. Dreams like that are dangerous.

"This is too generous, Alexei. As per usual with you."

He turns to face me, frowning as he sets his mug on the coffee table. "I'm far from being generous right now, Ryleigh. I don't want you working there at all. But it's a subject I'm guessing you're not ready to discuss."

"I can't quit, Alexei. What would I do for money? And don't you dare suggest that I continue relying on you. You know I hate it. It makes me feel cheap and useless, and I won't do it. You hardly know me. You have no obligation toward us."

He stalks closer with his eyes locked on mine, like he's a predator and I'm his prey, and rubs his large hands up and down over my shoulders. "I know enough. I know that you're self-reliant and independent. And I love that about you. Ninety-nine percent of the women I meet are happy to let me pay their way. You want to stand on your own two feet, and I respect that. I respect you."

I finish folding the blankets and stack them neatly inside the laundry basket. It's been a huge blessing to have a washer and dryer here. My apartment doesn't have one, and shuffling a baby out in the cold to a laundromat several times a week isn't my idea of fun. That's a reality I'll have to face soon enough—well, as soon as I can get my back rent paid up.

"Can I ask you something?" he says.

"Of course." After I move Ella to a blanket on the floor, I walk to the counter and pour myself a cup of coffee.

"If you didn't work there, what would you like to be doing instead?"

That's easy. "I always wanted to be a teacher. I finished my first two years of college on scholarship and with loans from my parents. Then the accident happened, and my parents . . ." I stop for a moment, looking down at my toes. "I lost my focus, I guess, and with it, my scholarship. That was two years ago now. I'd love to go back and finish my degree. But I make good money at the club, and now with Ella . . ."

He nods. "I get it. But for what it's worth, I think you'd make a wonderful teacher."

I smirk and mutter, "Thanks." His words wrap around me like a warm blanket, comforting me and giving me hope at the same time.

• • •

After breakfast and a shower, Alexei drove me to my place so I could pick up my car. I also managed to sweet-talk my landlord into opening my apartment so I could pack up some of my belongings, and get more clothes for Ella and me. He agreed, but only after I handed over several hundred dollars toward my back rent. Then I spent six hours in my underwear serving cocktails to men.

When I finally arrive home, the first thing on my agenda is a long, hot shower to wash the grime and regret off of me. Alexei gave me the code to his underground parking garage, and as I ride up the elevator, I smile, my anticipation at seeing the two of them bigger than you can imagine. The doors open, and nothing could have prepared me for what I find.

The first thing I notice is the classical music playing. Interesting choice. The second thing I notice is the aroma of roasting chicken. It smells delicious.

"Alexei?" I call out, not seeing them in the kitchen or living room.

"In the bedroom," he calls, already heading down the hall toward me.

"Where's Ella?"

He grins at me and places a tender kiss on my forehead when he gets close. "Sound asleep." He chuckles like this amuses him. "I'd like to get her on a regular schedule that doesn't include a nap right at dinnertime, but for now, it is what it is."

I follow him into the kitchen, more than a little amazed he's even thought about her schedule, let alone the fact that he'd like to make improvements to it. Why does that make my belly tingle?

"But she's been awake for the last several hours," he says, checking on something inside the oven. "As she grows, that time frame will eventually increase."

I nod, accepting the wineglass he hands me like this all makes perfect sense. When did this big, strapping jock become a 1950s housewife?

I blink and take a sip of the chilled white wine he's handed me.

"Welcome home." He smiles.

My insides twist. This isn't my home. Ella isn't our baby. None of this is real and playing make-believe like this is dangerous.

"Thank you," I murmur, my eyes on Alexei's.

"You want to take a shower before dinner?" he asks. "There's time."

"Sure." I take another sip of my wine and set the glass on the counter before making my way to the guest bath.

My knees are trembling, and it's not from the wine. It's from the drop-dead sexy man who's babysat all day, cooked me a hot meal, and was thoughtful enough to remember that I like a shower when I get home from work.

What am I going to do when it's time to leave this fairy tale and return to the real world?

I don't even want to think about that tonight. And if I'm being brutally honest with myself, I don't want to think about that *ever*.

• • •

After my shower, I dress in a pair of leggings and a tank top that hugs my curves. I apply moisturizer and light makeup, even taking the time to dry my hair so it falls in soft waves over my shoulders. I hate how I feel so dirty and grimy when I leave work, and now I feel fresh, clean, and worthy of the man who is waiting on me down the hall. Smiling one last time at my reflection and giving my hair a fluff, I head off.

I find Alexei where I left him in the kitchen. He watches me approach, a dark and predatory look on his face. I like it way too much. It sends a shiver all the way through me.

"Hi," he says, his voice tense.

"Hey," I say, attempting a casual and breezy tone.

The truth is, he makes me feel anything but casual. He makes me feel hot and irritated at times, but also cherished, and it's a feeling I'm not accustomed to at all. The truth is, his caring for me makes me nervous. What will I do if he changes his mind tomorrow and decides we're too much work? I won't let myself be devastated. I can't.

I consider asking him about his choice in music tonight, but I have a feeling he'd say something about classical music being good for babies, that it increases their IQ or something. It's a statistic I think I've heard somewhere. He's like a freaking baby-whisperer.

Alexei sets the table while I retrieve my wineglass. There are two whole roasted chickens, baked potatoes with all the fixings, and steamed broccoli. It's better than I've eaten in a long time. This is a far cry from my usual dollar-menu fare from the drive-through I often have for dinner. I don't want to tell him as much, as I sense it will only make him angry—or sad—and I can't bear either of those looks from him.

"This is amazing," I say instead, sitting in the chair he pulls out for me.

The other times we've eaten dinner together have been at the breakfast bar or on the couch. This feels like something different, and it makes my mouth twitch with a smile. I busy myself with cutting the chicken he serves me, and heap sour cream onto my steaming potato.

I don't even comment on the fact that he's made two chickens. I'm coming to learn his excessive caloric intake is necessary to maintain his body weight. The guy can eat, that's for sure.

"So . . . what did the guys say when you brought Ella with you today?" I smirk, blowing on a bite of my food before placing it in my mouth. *Yum!*

Alexei grins. "Fuckers thought she was mine."

I'm smiling. Why am I smiling? "Did it go okay? Was she good?"

He nods. "As good as a two-month-old can

be in public. She had a blowout when we first got there."

"A blowout?"

"She shit herself all the way up her back," he says, deadpan.

I almost choke with laughter before quickly swallowing my food. "Right. Sorry I asked."

He shrugs. "It was no big deal. I brought extra diapers and another outfit, so we were golden."

Oh my God, the image of Alexei with a diaper bag on his broad shoulder . . . ovary explosion times a thousand.

"Plus, my friend Jane, she's the assistant manager for the team, helped out. She took Ella while I was in the meeting."

I nod, giving him the side-eye as I ponder who the hell *Jane* is.

"This is delicious, by the way," I say, helping myself to another big bite.

"Thanks," Alexei says, but I can tell he has more on his mind than our dinner. "So, um, her mother . . . do you have any news yet?"

I release a heavy sigh and shake my head.

"Nothing yet. I called the officer I filed a report with, but there's still no news." *At least she hasn't turned up dead.*

We finish the rest of our meal and wash the dishes together.

Ella still isn't up from her nap when we settle on the couch. I've polished off one glass of wine and Alexei has refilled my glass, though he isn't drinking. I suspect it's because he has practice tomorrow. Something inside me likes how disciplined he is, while the other part of me feels a little weird drinking alone.

"How was work?" Alexei asks, sitting across from me. I can't help but notice his voice is a little cold when he asks this question.

"It was fine." I sip my wine.

"Anyone bother you today?" His darkened blue eyes, that beautiful midnight color I love, are watching everything, and I don't miss the way his gaze lingers, moving from my eyes down to my breasts.

I swallow. "Nope." Not any more than usual, anyway.

"Good."

His firm tone makes my insides quiver. It's quiet and dark outside, and we're alone, and I can't help but think about last night . . . about the way his hot mouth felt moving over my sensitive flesh . . . about the soft grunts he made when I took him deep in my throat.

"What is it?" he asks, his voice mischievous.

"What?" I blink at him innocently.

"You turned all pink on me. What's going on?"

Oh, dear God. "I was just . . . remembering last night."

Did I just say that out loud?

I can't believe I just admitted that.

He moves closer and takes my wine, setting it on the coffee table in front of us. "Come here, baby," he murmurs, his voice soft.

It does things to me. This big, strong man being sweet, so soft and tender . . . *so perfect.*

Don't, Ryleigh. I try to remind myself to guard my heart, but I fail miserably.

As I move closer to Alexei on the couch, he tilts my jaw and steals a sweet kiss, pressing his full mouth to mine.

"Missed you," he murmurs.

He shouldn't say things like that to me. We hardly know each other. *Right?* But there's no denying that raising a baby together for the past week has accelerated things between the two of us. He may just know me better than anyone . . .

D*on't think, Ry.*

And I don't.

I let Alexei kiss me until I'm writhing against him, making tiny, need-filled sounds.

When he suggests, "Let's go to my bedroom," all I can do is nod.

T*hank you, yes. Praise the Lord.*

Warm from the wine, I let Alexei tug me up from the couch. He guides me down the hall, his large hands on my hips the whole way.

When we enter his bedroom, it's dark and smells like him, and my knees immediately go weak. I swear I'm like one of Pavlov's dogs as I start salivating, thinking about taking him in my mouth again.

We stop in front of the bed, facing each other. The moment is quiet and intense and filled with such promise. His eyes are smoldering on mine, that's the only way to describe it and my insides tighten.

"Take this off." I lift Alexei's shirt and press my hands flat against his abs, thinking I'll never get used to how defined and firm they are. *It's a six-pack of heaven.*

He chuckles. "Yes, ma'am."

His shirt drops at our feet, and dear Lord, he's so sexy. All those hours spent lifting weights have paid off. Sculpted muscles over broad shoulders, a trim waist, and a body that makes that coveted *V*, which makes my gaze travel south of its own accord. *Pure perfection.* It's almost too much for me.

Well, almost . . . but not quite.

"I couldn't stop thinking about you today," he admits.

That makes two of us.

Before I have a chance to respond, he tugs my tank top off over my head, and then pulls my leggings down my legs, along with my panties, and soon I'm completely bare.

My heart pumps faster.

"Your turn," I murmur, reaching to unbuckle Alexei's belt.

He watches me with that amused expression I've come to love.

When his pants and boxers are pushed down and then off, I can't help but drop to my knees. And trust me, I'm not an oral sex kind of girl. I'm a *him* kind of girl, and his perfect cock begs to be licked and sucked.

"Baby," Alexei says, as if to stop me, his hand on my jaw.

I grin up at him. "Hush. I want to."

He lets out a deep groan as I fit my mouth around his rigid length and give it a generous kiss.

"Fuck," he growls as I take him deeper.

I can't get enough of him, and my hand strokes what I can't fit into my mouth.

"It's so good. Yes. Fuck."

I meet his eyes and see that his attention is focused on me too. I continue to treat him to wet kisses that earn me plenty of praise, until Alexei's hands find my upper arms and he hauls me to my feet.

"Enough. I want to be inside you. Please tell me you want this too. Do you want this, Ryleigh, me inside you?" His voice is so perfectly rough and desperate for me.

I nod, suddenly speechless.

"You sure? We don't have to. We could do what we did last night . . ."

I shake my head. "I want to. I'm more than positive."

Then I'm laid down in the center of his bed, and Alexei moves over me. He kneels between my parted thighs and raises one of my legs, curving it around his hip.

I watch his eyes. They're so intense. This moment means more to me than it should, but I can't help myself. Alexei sheaths himself in a condom while I watch. It's sexy how confident and sure he is.

He fits the head of his thick cock against my entrance and nudges forward. "Take a deep breath for me. This might be a tight fit." He grins wickedly, and I raise my eyebrows.

I do as he says, inhaling deeply as Alexei presses forward. I almost buck beneath him.

Holy shit. I knew how well-endowed he is, but nothing prepared me for *this*.

His long, thick cock slides inside me, claiming every inch of me, and makes my body clench with an even greater need. I don't know where he ends and I start.

"Alexei . . ." I moan once he's fully seated.

"Yes. Say my name when I fuck you."

I groan as he pulls back, grieving the loss of him.

But then he's moving, his hips snapping forward again and again, and *oh my God.* I can't help the cries that tumble from my lips.

"Alexei, yes," I moan.

He's so big . . . so commanding . . . so sexy with a scent that is so undeniably *him*.

"That's it, baby."

He grips my ass cheek in one strong hand, using my body to pull me onto his cock again and again, just the way he likes it. Part of me can't even believe that we're doing this. The other part of me can't believe that we were able to wait this long.

I throw my head back against the pillow, lost

in pleasure.

"Need you to come for me," he says on a groan.

I move my hips against his and Alexei brings a hand between us, rubbing my clit in firm circles as he continues to fuck me.

That's all it takes to thrust me over the edge.

My release rips through me with such ferocity that I'm breathless as I cling to his shoulders. Heat blooms in my core, my body milking his as my vision blacks out.

"Oh God, Alexei . . ."

"Fuck, baby. Yes." He groans, clutching my body close.

I sense the moment he falls over the edge with me, his long, thick cock pumping hot semen into the condom as he clings to me, kissing my neck and murmuring dirty words of praise in my ear.

When it's over, part of me can't even process what just happened. Alexei merely folds me into his arms and rolls over onto the bed, breathless, still holding me.

Holy. Shit.

That was by far the best sex I've ever had.

Alexei may have ruined me for anyone else. And, I'm not even mad.

CHAPTER
Eight

Alexei

I slap Ryleigh lightly on the butt to wake her, unable to keep my hands off those curvy ass cheeks of hers. Though I know I should demonstrate control, it's the last thing I want to do.

"Hmm?" she murmurs, blinking open hazy eyes.

"Time to get up, baby." I smile. I fucking love the sight of her in my bed; I can't help it.

"Why?" She groans.

It's only seven, so I get it, but I rouse her again. "I've got practice."

"Mmm." She makes a noise, but I'm not sure

what it means. It could mean *fuck you*. Or *go make me coffee*. It could also mean *okay, sounds great*.

I chuckle and swing my legs over the side of the bed. I head to the shower only because it helps wake me up, and not because I actually want to leave this woman in my bed.

Twenty minutes later, Ryleigh is still in bed, and trust me, I get it. She insisted on getting up with Ella both times last night, even though I told her I'd take care of the baby.

I head to the kitchen, intent on making her a strong cup of coffee, and possibly making myself a plate of eggs. Last night was incredible, and I'm more than a little proud that I've rendered Ryleigh so useless this morning. The caveman in me is beating his chest proudly.

I smirk as I flip on my coffee machine and watch the drip brewer begin to work. I already have a bottle ready for Ella on the counter, knowing she'll be awake in the next twenty minutes.

When I return to the bedroom five minutes later with a mug of steaming coffee for Ryleigh, she sits up in bed and smiles at me.

"You're my hero."

There's something about that smile and the way she says that—it hits me right in the chest and I want to hit replay on this moment.

"You're very welcome." I press a soft kiss to her lips. "Last night was incredible. You are incredible."

Ryleigh blushes and looks down.

She can't be shy now. Not after last night.

I lift her chin. "Tell me what you're thinking."

She meets my eyes at last. "I loved every minute of it."

I can't help but feel proud of how I pleased her. I skim my hands along her upper arms up to her neck, her face, and then tilt her mouth to mine. I steal a long kiss, which Ryleigh gives me freely.

My cock twitches to life, stirring between us.

"Do you have time for this?" she asks between kisses.

"I'll make time," I say, and she swats at my upper arm. "I mean it. I want you so bad, baby."

Without a word, Ryleigh draws her boxer shorts down over her hips and takes them off, leaving her bare from the waist down, and I remove her shirt.

God, she's sexy. Her tits are full and round, and I want them in my mouth right now.

I lean closer and pull her nipple between my lips. Ryleigh makes a need-filled sound unlike any I've heard before, and my cock bucks in my shorts. I rise from the bed and strip in about three seconds, and then I rejoin her, lifting her calf around my hip.

"Need to be inside you," I groan when my bare cock makes contact with her hot, wet pussy.

"I'm clean. On birth control," she murmurs.

Fuck.

"Me too."

She raises her eyebrows with a hint of amusement at my response, because it sounded like I was saying I'm on birth control too.

"The clean part," I say, clarifying. "I've been tested."

She smiles.

"I don't think male birth control has been cleared by the Food and Drug Administration yet," I add brilliantly.

God, shut up, Alexei.

Ryleigh only grins. "Less talking. More fuck-ing."

Or more specifically, bare-back fucking.

I press forward and groan at how incredible she feels. Warm. Wet. Snug.

And gripping me like her life depends on it. Heaven.

"Yes," she says on a groan. "Oh God."

"Hold on, baby," I tell her, placing her arms around my neck.

Ryleigh's smile fades away as I fuck her in long, deep thrusts. Pleasure-filled cries pierce the air as I move within her. She's perfect.

I'm so close. But I can't come before she does.

Correction: I *can* come just from looking at this woman, but I *won't* come until she's screaming my name.

I hike her leg higher around my waist, and the new angle does something for Ryleigh, not to men-tion that it puts me even closer to finishing myself off.

"Fuck. Alexei!" she cries, contracting around me in a mind-altering orgasm that is more powerful than anything I've ever felt from any woman . . . in my entire life.

I can't help but follow her over the edge, my own release powerful and unending.

H*oly shit.*

Finally spent, I collapse on top of Ryleigh. As she begins laughing, Ella whimpers from the other room. Perfect. Fucking. Timing.

A single thought flashes through my brain—

T*his is the most perfect way to wake up.*

CHAPTER
Nine

Ryleigh

lexei's still at practice. I've showered, straightened the apartment, and am now sitting on the floor playing with Ella. On one of his last shopping trips, Alexei picked up a couple of stuffed animals and a baby rattle, and I'm having a blast making this little baby smile, and getting such a kick out of the cute noises she makes as she plays.

Ella brings the stuffed pig to her face, gripping it in both chubby hands, and I smile down at her. I can't believe I've had her for almost two weeks already. I'm starting to feel a little more sure of myself around Ella, and a part of me knows that that assurance is because of Alexei and his confidence around babies. He calms me . . . centers me, even. He makes me think that maybe, just maybe I can do this.

As I look down at Ella, I can't help but think about Andi. I didn't know her for very long, but she was a good roommate. She was respectful of my personal space and paid her portion of the rent on time. We weren't friends, more like acquaintances who shared a living space. We didn't hang out often, but we were friendly enough. For a while, it was a mutually beneficial relationship that worked well. And then all that started to change. She was late on the rent a couple of months, and then she left one day, moving out without warning.

I didn't know she was pregnant or even why she moved out, but she must have been at least a couple of months along by then.

She showed back up out of the blue with Ella many months later. She looked so skinny, far too thin for having just had a baby, and all she said was that they needed a place to crash for the night. Mostly I was just surprised to see her, especially with a brand-new baby in tow, so much so that I blindly agreed. Now I wonder if it was all a plot to leave Ella with me. Because by the time I woke up the next morning, Andi was gone and Ella was crying, needing to be fed.

Where are you, Andi? I can't help but think she's in some kind of trouble. Maybe the kind of trouble that she doesn't want to involve an infant. Either way, my heart breaks for Andi, but mostly for Ella, whose mother obviously abandoned her.

While I'm lost in thoughts of what happened to make Andi abandon her child, my cell phone chirping startles me, and I reach for it on the coffee table.

It's a text from Alexei.

```
This morning was fun.
```

I chuckle, my mood lightening with just that one sentence. He's right; sex with him is fun. It's lighthearted and happy, and I never once felt self-conscious or uncomfortable. He has this way about him that makes everything feel so effortless and easy and good.

```
                       I don't know . . .
```

I tease him, thinking about what to write next.

```
Your technique could use a lit-
                        tle work.
```

Satisfied with my snarky reply, I sit back on my heels and tickle Ella's belly with her toy.

```
Little—there's a word I've never
heard before.
```

The ass. Apparently, he's being snarky too. Yes, the man is hung like a damn horse, and he knows it. My cheeks warm as I remember our encounters, both last night and again this morning.

I wait for his reply, anticipating something more vulgar, like him saying *you didn't seem to mind when you were coming on my cock.* But Alexei's a gentleman, because his next message simply says, *Let's discuss it tonight after Ella's in bed.*

I quickly type out *deal*, smiling to myself.

Ella lets out a little whimper, and it's not one of the happy squeals she made while we played.

"Are you ready for your morning nap, little one?"

I lift her from her spot on the floor and bring her to my shoulder, where I gently rock her and pat her back. I've been trying to think more about her schedule, ever since Alexei told me she should have set nap and feeding times. She's been awake for a couple of hours now, and so I think she could be getting sleepy again.

I carry her into the guest room and pull the curtains to cover the windows, blanketing us in almost darkness. The room is cool, but not chilly. Perfect for napping.

I lay Ella down with her pacifier and decide I'll join her. I lie down in the center of the cozy bed and close my eyes, feeling content and at peace for the first time in a long time, even though my life is anything but.

CHAPTER
Ten

Ryleigh

After breakfast the next morning, Alexei lingers in the kitchen, looking down at the tile. "I, um, forgot I invited my friends Jane and Weston over for dinner tonight. But if you want me to cancel . . ."

I shake my head. "Why would you cancel? Of course it's fine." It's his house, after all. I'm only the houseguest currently crashing here. "I'll just take Ella, and we'll get out of your hair for a while so you can entertain."

His brows pinch together. "That's not what I meant. I don't want you to leave. Are you up for meeting some of my friends and hanging out for a while? Weston's the quarterback on the team. Jane works for the team, and she's also Weston's girl-friend."

I blink at Alexei. He wants me to meet his friends? "Oh. Um, sure. Of course."

His openness to share his home and his life with me is beyond confusing. Are we friends? Fuck buddies? Something more? Mentally, I shake my head, chasing away those thoughts. It's best not to get my hopes up for when this all inevitably goes south.

"You don't have to change your plans for me. I'm more than fine with hanging out. As long as they don't mind a baby at the party."

He chuckles and shakes his head. "Not a party. I'll grill burgers. We'll have a couple of drinks. It'll be casual."

"Sounds great. What time are they coming?"

"Seven."

I nod. It gives me plenty of time to get myself cleaned up to meet one of Alexei's teammates and his girlfriend.

A little while later, he heads out for practice, leaving me to wonder what his friends will be like. Wonder if they'll share amusing stories about the man I don't really know but am temporarily living with. Or worst of all, if they'll be hostile toward me and wonder if I'm trying to trap him into a relationship.

Either way, it should be interesting.

• • •

Alexei's friends are great. They're friendly and thoughtful, and aside from a brief widening of Weston's eyes and a quick inhalation from Jane when they met Ella and me, they made us feel welcome.

That doesn't mean I feel comfortable.

Part of me is still adjusting to being here with Alexei . . . to his million-dollar lifestyle, beautiful apartment, and how very different it is from my life.

Having his friends here—who are obviously wealthy and in love—only makes me feel even more in the spotlight. I'm single and with a baby in tow, living paycheck to paycheck.

Jane laughs at something Weston says, snapping my attention back to the present. I take a quick sip of my wine and set the glass on the counter where we're lingering. I laid Ella down for a nap a little while ago, and now I'm not sure what to do with myself. Part of me likes having her as a social buffer. Is that weird?

Alexei pulls open the sliding glass door and strolls back inside, carrying a plate to the sink. "The burgers are on."

His eyes meet mine, and I wonder if he can tell how out of place I feel. Probably not. I've smiled at the right times and laughed at their jokes. I even made it a point to ask about Jane's work with the team, and about Weston's thoughts on their chances for the playoffs. I barely heard their answers, but hey, I asked.

"Ryleigh?" Alexei asks, still watching me. "Can you help me with something?"

"Sure."

I follow him into the pantry, which is the size of a walk-in closet, complete with a wall of shelves built in for wine bottles. I have no idea what he needs help with, but if he wants me to take over cooking the entire meal, I won't mind.

"What's up?" I ask.

When he turns to face me, we're standing just inches apart. It's impossible not to notice the way he towers over me. With all his bulky muscle, he easily weighs over a hundred pounds more than me. Anytime we're alone like this, it's as though the air between us is charged.

He meets my eyes and places his hands on my shoulders, giving them a squeeze. "I just wanted to check on you. I know this is probably a lot. First, I dragged you here, and now I'm entertaining friends and you're along for the ride. Are you okay?"

Is he serious? He's worried about how I'm feeling? It's so unexpected that a lump of emotion momentarily lodges in my throat.

"I just don't want to be in the way," I manage to say.

His hands on my shoulders give me a firm squeeze. "You're not. Jane and Weston are cool, so please don't worry."

I nod. "And you did sort of drag me here, didn't you?"

Alexei chuckles, and when he meets my eyes again, I don't miss the way they smolder with unmistakable heat. "I didn't hear you complaining last night."

My mouth curls into a smirk. "We'd better get

back out there before your friends wonder what's happening in here."

He shrugs. "Let them wonder."

I love how he doesn't care what anyone thinks, that he's never been concerned with his image or what the media would say about someone like him hanging out with someone like me.

"Promise you're okay?"

I nod. "Promise."

We rejoin his friends, and soon dinner is ready and everyone sits at the table. The burgers are cooked perfectly, and they pair well with the salad and wine Jane and Weston brought. I'm glad I thought to make something for dessert later. Alexei said they had dinner covered, but my grandmother taught me the most amazing recipe for peach cobbler, and I haven't made it in years.

"This is great," I say, helping myself to another bite of the tomato-and-feta salad that Jane brought.

She smiles warmly at me again, yet I can't help but notice the curious glances she's been casting my way all evening.

As Weston and Alexei have an enthusiastic conversation about their odds of winning the next game, Jane gives me another smile. I would really love to know what she's thinking.

"Alexei, everything turned out perfectly," I say at a lull in conversation.

"Your name is Alexei?" Jane asks, her nose crinkling. "How did I not know that?"

He shrugs. "Everyone calls me Alex."

"Everyone except for Ryleigh," she adds helpfully.

My cheeks threaten to turn pink, and I take a big gulp of my ice water to temper the burn.

"So, are you two . . ." Jane looks between Alexei and me with her brows raised, leaving the rest of her sentence unspoken.

Part of me is relieved, but the other part kind of wants her to put Alexei on the spot, wants to hear him define what this is.

Two people sleeping together? *Check.*

But is it more? Or am I just a charity case to him that he'll see through until I'm on my feet again, or until Andi comes back?

Alexei dodges the question by lifting one shoulder and looking at me. The smirk on his full lips makes my stomach twist. *Why am I the only one who calls him Alexei?* From what he's told me, he and Jane have been friends for years.

I duck my head and head toward the kitchen— flee is more like it—mumbling something about taking the ice cream out of the freezer to thaw a bit.

"I'll help." Jane smiles at me as though she knows something I don't.

Once we're alone in the kitchen, I grab two cartons of vanilla ice cream and place them on the counter, and busy myself with locating the ice cream scoop in the utensil drawer.

"So . . . how long have you and Alexei been friends?" I ask.

Jane grabs some bowls from the cabinet. It doesn't escape my notice that she knows exactly which cabinet they're stored in. She thinks about my question. "About four years now, I guess."

I nod. "And you and Weston? How long have you been together?"

She smiles and shakes her head. "That one is much harder. We grew up together, high school sweethearts. And when he left, I hated him for years. Then he got drafted to the Hawks, and well . . . he slowly won me back over." She pauses, catching my eye. "Oh my God, you wanted a simple answer like two months or something, didn't you?" She places her hands over her face and groans.

I chuckle and shake my head. "It's fine. You don't have to censor yourself around me. I'm just some chick crashing the party."

Her lips press into a line. "I doubt you're just some chick, Ryleigh. I've never seen Alex have a woman around, unless it was his mother or sisters. There was a time a couple years ago. Let's just say I know he wasn't a monk, but it's been a while since I've heard about anyone let alone a 'real' someone."

Butterflies zip nervously around my stomach. Her words light something inside me. Still, what we have can't be serious—it just can't. We've known each other a matter of days.

"So," I say as I begin scooping generous amounts of peach cobbler into each bowl. I'll be surprised if I don't gain five pounds staying here. "Alexei and I haven't known each other long, but he seems . . ."

I'm fishing for information, but Jane doesn't seem offended. Thankfully, she seems all too happy to play my game.

Leaning one hip against the counter, she peels the lids off the ice cream cartons and scoots them closer to me. "He's the best. He deserves someone amazing, you know?"

I nod. I agree completely. "He's been single for a while then?"

She doesn't even pause to think about it. "Yep."

"And you and he never . . ." My cheeks heat, and I pray she's not offended that I asked her that. But I'm too curious not to. They get along so well.

She breaks into laughter, shaking her head. "God, no. I mean, he's cute, don't get me wrong. And a big teddy bear, but no. We were always just friends. We didn't have the spark, or chemistry, or whatever. Plus, before Weston, I had a rule of never dating players on the team where I worked, so I never even considered it."

Relieved, I smile. "Makes sense, I guess."

It gives me a strange sense of comfort to know they never hooked up. I don't think I could handle standing here making small talk and serving dessert to a girl Alexei has slept with.

After I finish adding scoops of ice cream on

top of the servings of warm, gooey cobbler, Jane helps me carry the bowls and spoons into the dining room. I just hope I can survive dessert without making an ass of myself in front of Alexei's friends.

• • •

Later, when all the dishes are done and Alexei's friends are gone, and Ella has been bathed, fed, and tucked into bed for the night, the apartment is completely dark and quiet.

I've changed into my pajamas and just finished brushing my teeth when I pass Alexei in the hallway.

It isn't very late, but after cleaning up from the party and getting Ella down, we're both ready for bed, by the looks of it. He's dressed in a pair of loose-fitting gray sweatpants and nothing else.

"Where do you think you're going?" His hand on my waist stops me. He gives me a gentle tug backward until I meet the firm wall of his muscled torso.

"To bed?"

"Yes. In here, baby." His deep, warm voice sends trembles running through me.

I certainly didn't want to assume that I was going to be sleeping in Alexei's bed from now on, but this is a welcome detour.

Alexei's hands on my waist guide me to his bedroom. The lights are off, and it's almost too dark to make him out clearly.

But I don't need lights to know he's the sexiest man I've ever seen. Between the rumble of his low, sure voice, the broad expanse of warm muscle under my fingertips, and the way he always seems to put my needs first . . . let's just say I'm fairly certain after this morning that Alexei has ruined me for other men.

Desiree would lose her mind if she knew that in addition to being a badass football player, he's also good with babies and is an amazing lover. I decide I'd better keep that information to myself. Otherwise, she's liable to kidnap him in his sleep.

Scratch that, no one would ever be able to kidnap Alexei. That's another thing I like about him— I feel so safe here. I know that with him around, nothing bad will happen to me. I can just picture him facing down a bad guy or a bill collector, and saying, "Not on my fucking watch."

Alexei tilts my chin up toward his. "What are

you thinking about?"

I place my hand on his waist and move closer. "You."

He smiles. "Good answer."

Bending down to close the distance between us, he presses a tender kiss to my lips.

"Why do I call you Alexei, but your friends don't?"

He nuzzles my neck, kissing the sensitive spots he finds there. "Hmm?"

"Jane and Weston. They seemed surprised I don't call you Alex."

He lifts his head and meets my eyes. "I don't know. Everyone on the team calls me Alex."

All of America calls him Alex. He's known only as Alex Ivan. He doesn't give me an explanation for why he introduced himself as Alexei, but I can only think it was perhaps because he wanted a more intimate connection with me. At least, that's what I'm telling myself as he shoves my pajama pants down my legs, then lifts me and places me carefully in the center of his bed.

"Damn, you're sexy," he murmurs, palming my

breasts as he lies down beside me. He's definitely a boob man. Whenever my shirt comes off, he can't seem to help caressing my breasts, palming their weight in his hands, or sucking my nipples into his talented mouth.

Our conversation is apparently over, but it doesn't stop me from wondering about what all this means, even as Alexei's mouth moves lower and my worries morph into pleasure.

CHAPTER
Eleven

Alexei

N ow that I know how perfect Ryleigh feels writhing beneath me, how deliciously tight she is, the sounds she makes during sex that drive me insane, I'm having a hard time keeping my hands to myself and my dick in my gym shorts.

It's entirely inappropriate, yes. I know I promised myself I'd be a gentleman and that I'd help her because it's the right thing to do, not because I want something from her. Expecting physical pleasure in exchange for being a nice guy, thinking she'd share her body with me just because I gave her a warm place to sleep? That would make me no better than the creepy pricks who hassle her at work.

"So, what are you in the mood for?" Ryleigh asks, opening the fridge and peering inside.

Her ass looks so sexy in the yoga pants she's wearing, that it's instinct when I step up behind her and take her hips in my hands, tugging her back toward me.

"This," I murmur, kissing the back of her neck.

She chuckles and arches into me, bringing her curvy ass directly in line with my growing cock.

For once, food isn't the only thing on my mind, and since Ella is enjoying one of her late-afternoon naps, I figure we can delay dinner for a little while longer.

I bring my lips to the back of Ryleigh's neck and press a tender kiss there. "I couldn't stop thinking about you at practice."

"Mmm," she murmurs, her soft curves teasing me.

"Have you ever tried running forty yards with an erection?" I whisper against her neck.

Ryleigh chuckles. "Can't say I have."

My hands move from her hips to her perky tits, and I groan when I fill my hands with them. When my thumbs run over the firm peaks of her nipples, Ryleigh lets out a soft moan.

"You hungry?" I ask as the fridge door closes on its own.

She rocks her ass against me again, finding the ridge in my pants and grinding against it. "Yes, but not for food."

I smile. *Perfect.*

My palms slide from her breasts down over her stomach, and I dip a hand under the elastic band of her yoga pants. Pushing my fingers inside her panties, I apply light, teasing pressure as Ryleigh arches and moans into my touch. She's already getting wet.

"You get me so hard, baby. You feel that?" I shift my hips and rub my steely erection against her ass.

After one more naughty thrust between her perfect ass cheeks, I spin her in my arms and take her mouth in a hot, searing kiss. Ryleigh matches my enthusiasm, her tongue moving with mine.

I'm about three seconds away from lifting her to the kitchen counter and taking her right here when my intercom system beeps at us.

Ryleigh pulls back, confusion painted all over her lust-filled features. "What's that?"

Shit. It must be someone in my family. They're the only people the security staff is instructed to let in.

I pull a deep breath into my lungs and cross the room to the screen mounted on the wall. I tap a button. "Yes?"

"Alexei. It's Valerie."

Fuck. I press the button to let her in, then turn to meet Ryleigh's confused expression. "It's my little sister."

I have just enough time to adjust my cock in my boxers before the door bursts open to a crying seventeen-year-old.

"It's official," she chokes out between sobs. "I hate all men."

I open my arms and Valerie charges me, coming in for a hug and then crying against my chest. Ryleigh's eyes widen as she watches us.

When I clear my throat, Valerie steps back. "Oh. I didn't know you had company."

I nod. "This is my friend Ryleigh. She and Ella

are hanging out for a bit. That okay with you?"

"Ella?" Valerie asks, her thin brows rising.

Ryleigh crosses the kitchen and offers Valerie her hand. My sister quickly wipes at her cheeks before shaking Ryleigh's hand. "It's nice to meet you, and yeah, Ella is a baby I'm, um, babysitting for a little while."

Smooth. And probably a bit easier than getting into the truth right now.

Valerie seems to buy it, and nods before turning to face me again. "Seriously, though, your species is fucked up, Lex."

"Language, Val." I frown. "And men are not a separate species."

"They might as well be," she snaps back.

I lead her to the couch, and we sink into the cushions side by side. "Come tell me all about it. You hungry?"

She shrugs.

"Ryleigh and I were just discussing dinner. Stay and eat. And then you can tell me whose ass I need to kick." I flex my biceps for good measure.

This gets a smirk out of Valerie, followed by a

dramatic sigh. "Tempting offer . . ."

"You want to eat with us or what?" I ask again. I'm always hungry, but it is dinnertime. If I send her home hungry, my mom will have something to say about that.

Valerie shakes her head. "I don't want to impose."

"You're not. We were just about to make something," Ryleigh says.

We were actually just about to squeeze in some sex before dinner too, but my sister doesn't need to know that. I'm pleased to see that Ryleigh's not thrown off or annoyed by this unexpected intrusion. Maybe she's just curious to see me in big-brother mode.

"Actually, let's order takeout so you don't have to cook."

Ryleigh nods. "Whatever you guys want. I don't mind either way."

I grab the stack of takeout menus I keep in the kitchen drawer and hand them out to the girls. "Thai. Mediterranean. Japanese. Italian. Mexican."

"Mexican," they both say at once.

I call in the order on my phone and settle back down beside Valerie. Even though she's putting on a brave front, for her to drive over here means something's really wrong.

"So, tell me what happened," I say.

Valerie looks down, picking at her thumbnail. "What kind of asshat breaks up with someone right before the winter formal? Now I don't have a date to the dance."

I rise to my feet. What a punk ass kid. "I'll go talk to him, set him straight."

She grabs my arm and gives it a tug. "Oh no, you don't."

I look over to Ryleigh, and she's biting back a grin. I recall then the fact that she's an only child and has never had someone to play the concerned older brother for her.

Releasing a heavy exhale, I drop back onto the couch beside my youngest sister. She's changed so much these last couple of years after discovering makeup and boys. You'd think that since I already went through this with my other two sisters, I'd be used to the drill. But when I look at Valerie, I still see the skinny, annoying seven-year-old she was when I moved out of the house ten years ago. I'm having a hard time adjusting to the fact that she's nearly a grown woman.

"We'd only been out a couple of times, but I was happy knowing I had someone to go to the dance with. I bought a dress and everything," Valerie says.

Ryleigh leans forward and places her hand on Valerie's. "Guys aren't everything. Trust me. My friends and I used to go to the school dances together, and we always had way more fun than our friends whose dates didn't like to dance."

"I like that plan," I say, smirking.

Valerie rolls her eyes. "Of course you do."

Ryleigh releases Valerie's hand and sits back. "I promise you'll still have fun. Probably more fun because you won't have to worry about if your date is having a good time."

Valerie thinks it over. "My friend Sara is going alone."

Ryleigh nods. "There you go."

Satisfied that the problem is solved, Ryleigh gets up with the intention of checking on Ella, if I had to guess, or maybe just to give us a minute alone.

Valerie shoots me a look, and I sense that she wants to ask more about who Ryleigh is and exactly what she's doing staying here. It's rare for me to have a woman here, and I'm sure it's nothing Valerie's ever seen before.

But since I'm not ready to answer any questions about that yet, I pull her in for a quick hug. "You okay now?"

She nods. "I'm fine now." Then she raises her eyebrows dramatically a few times. "So, Ryleigh? Spill it, bro. I need deets."

"Shut it. Let's eat, yeah?"

She purses her lips and pouts.

"No more questions, and I'll take you out for ice cream later."

"Gelato, and you have a deal," Valerie says, smiling.

As if I could say no to that. "Deal."

CHAPTER
Twelve

Alexei

Valerie, that little freaking snitch. Of course she rushed right home and told my mother I have a girl living with me.

And less than three days later, here we are on my mother's doorstep in the suburbs to "have dinner," which is code for my family getting to meet Ryleigh and my mother to scope her out and decide if she's good enough for her son.

Just fucking great.

Ryleigh has enough going on. I really didn't want to subject her to my family and all their questions until—well, I don't know when. But certainly not now, not until things calm down some.

The front door swings open, and with it, a burst of warm air.

Ryleigh fidgets nervously beside me, and I place my hand against the small of her back. While I'm not as nervous as she is, I'm definitely a little overwhelmed at the idea of dealing with my mother right now.

My mother, dressed in a gray sweat suit, frowns as her gaze moves past me to Ryleigh and Ella, the line between her brows deepening. "Who is this?"

And she doesn't say it as a breezy, easygoing who's this? It comes out in her thick Russian accent, sounding a lot more like who the fuck is this girl trailing after my son, and why in God's name does she have a baby I know nothing about?

Shit. This is going to fucking suck.

I lean close to my mother and whisper, "Breathe, Ma, you invited us here. And be nice."

Her lips press together and she ushers us inside. "Come in, it's freezing. And you have a little one."

Ryleigh grins, oblivious to the tension between my mother and me, thank God. Once we're inside, she pushes the fuzzy blanket down that was protecting Ella's head from the cold, and my mom leans closer to take a peek.

"Oh, she's brand new. Very precious, *printsessa*," she coos, gently combing her fingers through Ella's wavy blond hair.

I chuckle as I watch my mom interact with her. She's a grandmother six times over, a role she loves and excels at, but her youngest grandchild is almost a year old now. I have a feeling we'll face some tough questions tonight, but I also predict that my mom will be holding Ella close and singing to her in Russian at some point too. She may come across as a hard-ass, but she has a major soft side, and babies are her number one weakness. Actually, now that I think about it, bringing home a woman to meet my mom for the first time, it might be genius of me to bring a baby along too.

I take a deep breath and steel myself for what's to come. "Mom, this is Ryleigh and Ella. And Ryleigh, this is my mother, Irina."

"It's so nice to meet you. Thank you for having us." Ryleigh smiles at my mom, taking it all in. She looks genuinely excited to be here. "Is this where you grew up?"

Ryleigh's gaze roams over the overstuffed bookshelves and the dusty photos hanging on the wall of my sisters and me from first grade through senior year of high school. It's embarrassing, but honestly, I don't care that Ryleigh's seeing it. I have an amazing family, and yeah, my mom is nuts, but she loves us. When we lost my dad my senior year of high school, it only made us all grow closer as we realized how precious our time together really is.

"Born and raised," I say proudly. Most pro-league players move around a lot, so I feel fortunate to live in the same city where my family lives. Who knows, I could get traded in the future, and if I do, I'll probably end up moving my entire family along with me. Valerie would throw a shit fit at leaving her friends, but whatever.

"This is so great. So homey." Ryleigh smiles again, shifting Ella's sleeping weight in her arms. I can tell she's truly impressed, and it makes my gut twist, wondering about her own family home life.

Two of my sisters appear from the hall, both with questioning looks as they take in Ryleigh and Ella standing there.

Yeah, this is going to be even more awkward than I realized.

I take a deep breath and try to smile in an at-

tempt to reassure Ryleigh. "Tracey, this is Ryleigh."
I nod to Ryleigh. "And you remember Valerie?"

Ryleigh reaches out a hand. "Yes, of course.
Nice to meet you. And good to see you again, Valerie."

My sisters each shake her offered hand and
take a moment to admire Ella just like Mom did.
But their confusion and uncertainty are obvious.
They want to know what the fuck is going on, and
I can't blame them. Are we dating? Is she living
with me? These are all good questions. Who does
Ella belong to? Too bad I'm fresh out of answers.

It isn't like me to bring a woman home. And
it's not like I called them and talked about Ryleigh,
or even told them I was seeing someone. This is all
coming as a complete shock. And to be honest, if
one of my sisters brought some random new guy
around, I'd probably act like a fucking asshole to
the dude. It's practically my job as a brother, especially since I'm the oldest.

"Where's Jase tonight? The kids?" I ask Tracey. It's way too quiet for her two- and three-year-
olds to be here.

"He took them to pick up ice cream for dessert.
They'll be back in a little bit."

I nod. So Ryleigh will really get thrown into the crazy tonight. I swear it's like my sister gives those kids caffeine.

"So, Ryleigh, do you want something to drink?" Tracey asks, her voice a little louder than necessary.

Ryleigh's eyes meet mine, and I give her a slight nod. "Go ahead. I'll take Ella."

Ryleigh places her into my arms and goes with my sister to the kitchen. Valerie follows them, leaving me alone with my mother.

Ma's face contorts as she stalks closer to press a finger into my chest. "Is she yours, Alexei? So help me God . . ."

This has been my mom's biggest fear since I was in high school. She always preached safe sex, and warned me about women who would want to trap me into parenthood and child support once I hit it big.

I shake my head. "She's not mine."

My mother physically sags with relief.

Some weird part of me wants to add, *But I wish she were.*

"Ryleigh is a woman I've started seeing. She's amazing, Ma. And Ella's mom split, so Ryleigh stepped up. It's complicated, but it's also not."

My mother's eyes widen, and she nods. "Come on. Your sisters are probably roasting her over an open flame right about now."

I grin. Mom doesn't know Ryleigh. She may look sweet and innocent, but trust me, she can hold her own. Even against my sisters.

CHAPTER
Thirteen

Ryleigh

I've just dumped a load of laundry onto my bed to fold and settled Ella onto her Boppy pillow on the bed beside the pile of clothes. I didn't realize how much I've missed having easy access to a washing machine. This is way better than hauling clothes to a laundromat. Ella lets out a little squeal of approval, mirroring my sentiments exactly.

"You might as well learn now." I smile at her.

Folding her clothes is a snap. They're so unbelievably tiny; I still don't think I'm used to it. I make a little stack of baby onesies and socks next to my leggings and sweatshirts. Then I smirk.

Somehow one of Alexei's T-shirts has gotten

mixed in with my load of laundry. I hold it up next to my body. It's enormous. The sight of it mixed in with Ella's stuff and mine makes me smile. He's at practice this morning—yes, I may have already looked at the clock at least seven times, already ready for him to be back home.

Last night went so much smoother than I imagined. Meeting his mother was nerve-racking, but once we started talking, I think I won her over. She seemed so surprised and impressed that I was caring for a baby who wasn't mine.

Ella makes a squeal of happiness, and I chuckle at her. "You're a good little helper, aren't you?"

I fold Alexei's shirt with care and place it onto the stack just as my cell phone rings. I grab it from the bedside table to answer.

It's Andi.

Holy shit. Finally.

My heart jumps. "Andi? Where are you?"

"I am so sorry. Is Ella okay?" She sounds tired and scared. It rattles something inside me.

My gaze drifts to Ella, where she lays on the bed. "She's fine. Where have you been?"

"I'll explain everything in person. Are you home?"

Hot shame burns through me. She trusted me with her baby, and now here I am homeless. But I can't tell her that. Not until I know what the hell is going on.

"No, actually. But I can meet you somewhere. The coffee shop on the corner near the apartment."

"Sure," she says.

"Give me twenty minutes."

We end the call and I pack up Ella, buckling her into her carrier with a fuzzy blanket, and wonder if this is the last time I'll do this. Trying to hold back tears as I look at her, tears for this little baby who's been under my care for the past two weeks, so much so that I'm starting to get attached to her. But I can do this. So I grab her diaper bag filled with all her stuff, and then look down at her angelic face.

"Come on, sweetie, we're going to see your mommy."

I think about texting Alexei to let him know I'm going out, and then decide against it. He probably won't see my text since he's on the practice field, and if he does happen to see it, he'll probably only worry. I want to see how all this will play out first, and then I'll call him later.

We arrive at the coffee shop, and Andi is already there. When I spot her across the room, my knees buckle. She looks even frailer than she did two weeks ago, and her hair is completely gone, at least as far as I can tell with the silk scarf wrapped around her head. Her face is pale, but her eyes light up when she sees us. She rises on unsteady feet, placing both hands flat against the table to help with her balance.

"Oh my God," Andi cries, reaching for Ella. "She looks so much bigger."

Still in a state of shock, I unbuckle the straps and lift Ella out, then hand her to her mother. "She's been eating well," I say.

Andi sits down with Ella in her arms, quietly stroking her smooth cheeks and downy hair while tears stream from her eyes.

I think I'm in a state of shock myself. Seeing her in this condition, I find all my unanswered questions start to come into focus. My heart breaks for Ella, for Andi, and for whatever this is that she's going through. It's such a tender moment that I don't dare interrupt, despite all the questions buzzing through my brain.

After several minutes, Andi wipes her cheeks and straightens in her seat. She's still holding Ella close to her chest, but her gaze is now fixed on mine. "Thank you so much for taking care of her while I was away. I'm sorry for just leaving, but I knew I could trust you to do the right thing. I couldn't bear to leave her to the system"

I nod, not quite knowing what to say. "Where were you? Is everything . . . okay?"

Andi looks down at her daughter and smiles sadly. There's a pause before she speaks. "I have cancer. Have had it off and on for about four years now."

"What? Oh my God, I never knew." I lean in closer, my eyes wide.

She nods. "I was in remission while we lived together. I hoped I would stay that way. But I have an aggressive form of brain cancer that's returned. It's called glioblastoma. The radiation I just had was sort of a last-ditch effort, but my body didn't respond well to it, so . . ."

She doesn't say anything else, and I suddenly understand why she left Ella with me—to go and get treatment in the hospital.

"They say I have one to three months left. I've been in the hospital because my health is so compromised from the treatments they gave me, but I checked myself out this morning."

I reach for her hand and she clasps mine tightly, weaving her fingers between mine.

"They want to move me to hospice right way. I told them I'd come back, but I had to get things in order with Ella first."

I nod, feeling numb.

Andi reaches into her oversized purse and pulls out a stack of paperwork. A check made out in my name is paper-clipped to the pages. It's for $2,406.12.

She hands me a pen and pushes the stack of papers toward me. "I know it's a lot to ask, but I know you'd take good care of her. I've seen how hard you work, the sacrifices you've made."

"I don't understand. What is all this?"

"Guardianship paperwork. I want to see if you'll agree to become Ella's legal guardian so she doesn't end up a ward of the state."

"You want me to adopt Ella?" I ask, my mouth suddenly dry. My entire world is spinning out of control right now. I don't want to say no but at the same time I can barely even pay rent for myself let alone take care of a child. I'm mad and confused and overwhelmed. She can't be serious. Only I'm pretty sure she is. Her expression is totally somber.

"Yes."

"There has to be someone else. Your parents?"

Andi shakes her head. She's an only child, like me, it was something we talked about having in common, but I realize I never heard her mention her parents.

"It's just my mom. I never knew my father. My mom kicked me out when I was sixteen because I didn't agree with her lifestyle."

"Her lifestyle?" I ask, realizing I'm still gripping her hand. I release my hold, and she moves her hand away to stroke Ella's hair again.

"Drinking. Drugs. A different boyfriend every week. I've been on my own since then. Finished high school, got a job. And then, well, you know." She gestures to herself.

"Maybe she's changed, gotten herself cleaned

up since then," I say, my voice shaky.

Andi shakes her head. "She hasn't. She lives in Boca now in some trailer park. I spoke to her on the phone recently. I won't have Ella raised like that. And I doubt my mom would take her. She never offered to help with any of my medical bills, never came up to take care of me when I was so sick from treatments all the other times."

That's awful. My parents aren't around either, and that's hard enough, but to know that your mom is still alive and just doesn't care—that's almost even more heartbreaking.

"And Ella's father?" I ask.

Andi looks down. "It was a one-night stand. I don't even know the guy's last name, to be honest."

Wow. This situation has escalated from bad to worse. I look down at the sweet little face I've come to love these past couple of weeks, and I know what I have to do.

I reach for the pen and sign my name on every single page while tears roll down Andi's cheeks, and my own eyes well up. There was never a choice not to keep her.

"Thank you so much. You have no idea what

this means to me."

I nod. "She's a great baby. I'll take good care of her."

Andi sniffs and wipes her face. Then she takes the paperwork, folds it back into her bag, and hands me the check. "This is all the money I have to my name. Take it. There's no way I'm giving it to the bill collectors."

"Can I bring her by the hospital, maybe later this week on my day off?" It's all I can even think of to ask right now.

Andi nods enthusiastically. "Yes, please. I'll text you my room number when they move me."

We sit there for another hour, enduring strange looks from the baristas, but it doesn't matter. This is a mother and baby saying good-bye. In a way, it's also me saying good-bye to Andi, as well.

It probably isn't their final farewell, but it is Andi's good-bye to all the hopes and dreams she had for this little girl. She won't be the one to braid Ella's hair or drop her off for her first day of school. She won't be the one to kiss her scraped knees or talk to her about boys. She won't be the one to watch her get married someday. But I will. And the emotion of that is hitting me hard. My life. . . Andi's life. . . baby Ella's life. . . all have been changed in an instant.

Now I understand why Andi did things the way she did. If she'd come to me and asked me to become the guardian of her daughter, I would have said *no way*. I knew nothing about babies, and would have said I wasn't cut out for this at all. But these past two weeks have shown me that maybe I can do this. Alexei's help has been amazing, but now knowing that I'm going to become a full-time parent, well, it changes everything.

I can't rely on his generosity forever, especially not for the next eighteen years, and it wouldn't be fair to him to expect that he would step into the role of dad just because we happened into his life. I have no idea if we're even compatible long term, and trying to date while I learn how to be a mom is probably a recipe for disaster.

It's not like he introduced me as his girlfriend when I met his family. The truth is, I really don't know where we stand, or what we are. It's been fun, but I guess the fun's over now.

I know what I have to do—for me and for Ella.

I won't saddle Alexei with my responsibilities. It's way too much to ask. He's practically a celebrity. He doesn't want to be dating someone with so much on her plate, or taking care of a baby that isn't his. Yes, we've had great sex, and yes, it will be hard to say good-bye to him, but I know the right thing to do is to let him off the hook. He didn't ask for this. But I made a promise to Andi, and I will never regret signing my name on those papers.

After I finish here, I'll drive over to Alexei's and pack up my stuff before he gets home. And then I'll pay the rest of the rent I owe with the money from Andi.

It's time to go home and be a real adult. It's time to become a single mom. It's time to say good-bye to the man who has come to mean everything to me, the knight in football armor who rescued Ella and me, and become a real grown-up. Again.

I can do this.

I have to.

CHAPTER Fourteen

Alexei

Thanks for everything.

I stare at the text message on my phone from Ryleigh, wondering what in the world is going on. I've just arrived home from a tough day on the field, and my house is empty. Completely fucking empty. Not only are they gone, but so is all their stuff. I don't like it one fucking bit.

I look at my phone again and decide to call Ryleigh. No surprise, she doesn't pick up. So I type out a message and hit SEND.

Where are you?

We went home. Figured it was
time.

What are you talking about?

I call her again and again, but she doesn't answer.

I just need a little space,
Alexei.

Is everything okay? Did I do
something wrong?

We had sex last night and again this morning,
and I can't help but think that maybe I rushed her
. . . rushed us. But she wanted to take this relationship further just as much as I did, didn't she?

*F*uck.

I scrub my hands through my hair.

Space. She needs space. Fine.

I'll be leaving in a few days for Miami, but I
need to see them first. Need to look into her eyes

and find out why the sudden change. As far as I know, I never made her feel unwelcome. I tried to be helpful and do what was right, just like how I was raised.

> Can we meet for breakfast tomor-
> row?

Ryleigh doesn't respond right away, and I wonder if she'll deny me even that.

I sink into the couch cushion and push my hands into my hair.

Fuck it.

I'm definitely getting drunk tonight.

I text a couple of my buddies from the team, knowing I'll need a distraction tonight to avoid putting my fist through a wall. Already, my apartment feels empty and way too quiet.

• • •

A while later, Weston and Colin are planted on my couch, fighting over some stupid video game, but it's better than being alone right now. A half dozen empty beer bottles are scattered across my coffee table, along with a couple of empty pizza boxes.

"You really that torn up over this girl?" Weston asks.

I give him the side-eye, and Colin breaks into laughter.

"Damn, dude. If looks could kill . . ."

I gave them the gist of what happened when they arrived, but only the basic details.

Weston holds up one hand. "Hey, man, I was just asking. It's not like you never hassled me about my relationship with Jane."

That much is true. I didn't believe he was capable of settling down into a monogamous relationship. He'd just had his heart broken by some chick, and Jane was . . . well, Jane. She's as serious as they come. And she's a close friend. I didn't want him fucking up and breaking her heart when he was just intending to blow off steam.

Thankfully, Weston knew enough to know that Jane wasn't some jersey chaser. She was the real deal, someone you could easily settle down with and share a life with. In fact, when I first met her, I kinda wondered if we'd cross over from friends territory into something more. But we never had that chemistry. I've always viewed her as only a friend.

I shake my head, clearing my thoughts, and realize Weston is still talking.

"You met her, what, a couple of weeks ago?"

I shrug. "Doesn't matter. I can't help how I felt. How I feel."

He's right that I haven't known her long, but we spent nearly all our time together, living together from day one. It probably forced us to grow closer than we would have otherwise. I know that she sleeps curled on her side, how she likes her coffee, that she likes to sing in the kitchen while she cooks. I know what her body feels like moving alongside mine, and how she becomes incapable of returning my kisses when she comes—her soft mouth parting while I nibble her lips with kisses as her toes curl.

"Fuck." I shove my hands into my hair. This isn't helping anything. "I need to be drunk. Right now."

Colin frowns and passes me the half-empty bottle of whiskey sitting on the table beside him.

"Sucks, dude," he says in consolation.

"Yeah." I bring the bottle to my mouth and take a long swig. I'm the only one drinking out of it anyway, why bother with a glass? My entire attitude tonight is basically fuck everyone, fuck everything. I'm trying to put on a brave front and not lose it in front of the guys, but the truth is, I'm so fucking close to the edge right now.

Maybe if I understood why Ryleigh left, what I did wrong . . . Maybe. Actually, scratch that, that probably wouldn't matter. I want her back. Her and Ella.

I know there's a lot of shit to work out, and yeah, it's nuts that Ryleigh's roommate just took off, but still. I liked being there for them, feeling useful, seeing the way she looked at me. It was different from the usual hero worship I get on the field. Ryleigh appreciated me for me. Who I am at my core. The fact that I grew up with sisters and know about babies. She liked feeding me, and never let me get away with anything. She held her own, and I really like that about her.

"So, what's the game plan?" Weston asks, a look of pity crossing his rugged features.

I squint at him. "Do you even fucking shave anymore? Just because you got engaged, dude—" I don't get to finish that statement before a throw pillow comes sailing past my head.

"Fuck you," he mutters.

I raise the bottle of whiskey. "I'll drink to that."

Colin grabs the bottle from my hand and re-caps it. "Enough of that. You'll be fucking useless tomorrow."

He's right. We have practice in the morning. None of us should be drinking, but I appreciate the fact that they're here for me.

"I asked her to meet me for breakfast tomorrow." I'll be done with practice early since tomorrow is special teams practice with the offensive co-ordinator. I'm usually only there until ten or so. It leaves plenty of time to meet her before her shift, if she's working.

"What'd she say?" Weston asks.

Just as I open my mouth to reply that she hasn't responded, my phone chirps from the coffee table.

Colin snatches it before I do. His face breaks into a smile. "We'd better get you to bed, prin-cess. You'll need your beauty sleep." I grab for my phone, but he continues holding it. "You've got a date with your girl in the morning."

She's not my girl, but I want her to be.

One step at a time. Time to get these goons out of my apartment.

CHAPTER
Fifteen

Alexei

Ryleigh sits across from me, her legs folded beneath her on the booth. She's rigid, and has barely looked at me. It stings more than I'd like to admit. She's dressed in a pair of leggings and an oversized sweatshirt that keeps falling off one shoulder, her hair is up in a messy bun like she couldn't be bothered with it, but she still looks so good that it hurts to know I can't reach over and touch her.

She finally responded to my text late last night and agreed to breakfast. After that, Weston and Colin left, and I tried in vain to sleep. Practice was a blur, and now I'm here.

My stomach is in fucking knots, and I hate everything about this. Ella rests next to her, still strapped into the baby carrier. I wish she'd cry, scream, do something, because at least then it would match how I feel right now.

I lean in closer. "Did I do something wrong?"

Ryleigh's eyes flash to mine. "No. Of course not. You've been incredible. More than I could have ever asked for."

The waitress chooses that moment to deliver the coffees we've both ordered.

"Thank you." Ryleigh reaches for her mug and dumps in a generous serving of sugar and cream.

The waitress flips open a notepad and looks at me. "What are you having?"

"Five eggs, over easy. Breakfast sausage. Two pancakes with bacon, and a side of wheat toast, please." My gaze swings to Ryleigh, who's stirring her coffee, staring at it intently rather than looking at me. "Ry?"

"Oh, nothing for me. Just coffee."

I shake my head. "You're eating. What do you want? Eggs? Pancakes?"

She rolls her eyes. "Fine. French toast, please. With a side of bacon."

Satisfied, the waitress flips her notebook closed and saunters away.

Ryleigh's got to get over this whole thing about me paying. I make millions, and it does me no good sitting in a bank account. I enjoy treating my friends and family. It pisses me off when she takes that away from me, and I think I've done everything I can to not make her feel like she and Ella are a financial burden.

I take a sip of my coffee, trying to compose myself. My chest feels tight, and I have no idea why I'm out of breath like I just ran a four-second forty.

Ella wakes suddenly, letting out a sharp cry.

Ryleigh flinches and turns toward the baby. She unbuckles the straps and carefully lifts her out. "She needs a new diaper."

I rise to my feet and reach for her. "I've got it."

Ryleigh frowns, but makes no move to pass Ella over.

I thrust my hands closer. "I said I've got it." Is she really going to rob me of this too? I didn't even get to say good-bye to Ella yesterday before they just took off.

Finally, Ryleigh relents and hands the baby to me. I shoulder the diaper bag and stalk off for the restrooms at the back corner of the restaurant.

Cradling the baby against my chest, I head into the men's room and find a dude at the urinals taking a piss, but no baby-changing station. *What the fuck?*

The guy flashes me a confused look, and I have no idea if it's because he's recognized me or because I'm holding a baby.

I huff out a frustrated sigh and exit, heading straight into the women's restroom. Thankfully, it's deserted, but even if it weren't, I'd like to see someone try to stop me from changing Ella. She needs a new diaper. And we need a changing table.

I open the changing table and wipe it down with an antibacterial wipe from the diaper bag, then lay down a small blanket and place Ella on top.

"You okay, princess? I'll get you cleaned up good as new."

She makes a soft cooing noise, and my throat tightens.

I unsnap her onesie and remove the soiled diaper, wiping her carefully like my older sister taught me the first time I changed her daughter. Once Ella's perfectly clean, I take out a new diaper and cover her.

"That's my girl." I grin down at her, snapping up the buttons on her pink onesie.

The words lodge in my throat. It's a lie. She's not my girl. And neither is Ryleigh.

But I intend to find out why, and what the fuck I can do about it.

"Let's roll, baby."

I lift her into my arms and head back into the dining room. Once we arrive at the table, I hand her to Ryleigh.

"She smells so much better now." Ryleigh smiles for the first time since she arrived, and it's not lost on me.

"She's perfectly clean," I say, sitting back down on my side of the booth.

Ryleigh passes me some hand sanitizer, which I gratefully accept, and then her eyebrows pinch together as she looks toward the restroom doors. "Did you change her in the women's room?"

I shrug. "There wasn't a changing table in the men's. Trust me, I'm going to say something to the manager when we leave."

Ryleigh's eyes widen and she takes a sip of her coffee, knowing better than to argue with me about this.

A silence descends upon us, and I can't help but want to cut to the chase—to get to the real reason why we're here. The waitress provided a nice distraction, and then Ella's diaper, but I need answers. Plain and simple.

"Can I ask . . . did something happen that made you leave yesterday?"

She sets her coffee mug down and finally meets my eyes. "I got in touch with Andi."

My heart starts to thump hard. "Yeah? That's good, right?"

Ella's still with Ryleigh, though, now seated in the carrier on the booth seat next to her. So, obviously that's part of whatever is going on. My stomach tightens.

She pauses, running her hands through her hair, stalling for time. "Andi has cancer. She's dying. And she asked me to be Ella's legal guardian."

Wow. That's a lot to take in. Not at all what I expected. I figured Andi couldn't handle being a mom and ran off. Fuck, this is so much worse. "What did you say?"

Ryleigh touches a stray lock of her hair that's escaped her loose ponytail. "I signed the papers. There's no one else. And the only other option for Ella is that she'd be a ward of the state. I couldn't bear the thought of abandoning her."

"I see." My heart clenches inside my chest. Damn. Ryleigh's so headstrong. So independent. So sweet. It's heartbreaking. "Still doesn't explain why you left."

Her gaze suddenly snaps up to mine. "I don't want to burden you. You've done enough."

I feel like I've been sucker punched. "You were never a burden to me, Ryleigh. Neither was Ella. You guys were all I thought about when I was gone those two days. And having you both around made me realize what I've been missing out on, living the bachelor life. You brought meaning to my days, and even though you're a pain in the ass," I smirk at her, "walking into the apartment last night and realizing you both were gone . . . fuck, it almost gutted me. I want you both to come back to my pla— I mean, our place."

Her mouth presses into a line. "I'd never ask that of you. We hardly know each other, Alexei."

That's bullshit, and she knows it. We know all the things that matter. I know what's in her heart, and she knows mine. Yeah, it's fast, but when you know, you know. Right? Isn't that what everyone always says?

But I don't say any of this. I take a second to compose myself, pulling a deep breath into my lungs. "I know you wouldn't ask, but I'm offering, Ry. There's a difference."

She swallows, still looking down. Still quiet.

Shit. I feel like I'm about to fucking beg her to come back. I've never begged a woman in my damn life. But there's something different about her, about our connection, and I'm not willing to give up on us. This could be the start of something real. It doesn't bother me in the slightest that she and Ella come as a package deal. The truth is, the baby has grown on me over the past couple of weeks. I want them both in my life.

"I also didn't want to assume you'd want to date someone with a baby. Pre-made family and all. Before, we both thought this was me temporarily watching Ella. Now, she's all mine, no take-backs, no returns."

"I'm a big boy. I can decide what I want, Ryleigh."

Her mouth twitches. "And what do you want?"

I lean closer. "I'm looking at it. I've never wanted two women in my life more than I do right now."

Ryleigh gives me a doubtful glance like she doesn't truly believe me, but she doesn't say a word. Our food is delivered before I have a chance to say anything else, and we dig in together.

"Mmm . . . this French toast is amazing." She cuts off a piece for me. "Try a bite?"

I grin. "Sure." She brings the fork to my lips, and I accept the bite. Warm maple syrup and the sweetness from the powdered sugar hit my tongue. "Delicious."

It's crazy how comfortable we are together. Anyone looking at us might think we're an old married couple. Why does that thought make me smile rather than cringe? It's so not like me, but everything with her just feels right.

Ella's still sound asleep by the time we finish. She really is a good baby. After I pay the bill, we go outside to the parking lot.

"I don't want to rush you, but I like having you guys close, and more importantly, safe. Come home with me?" *Permanently*. I don't say that last part, but we'll get there. I hope.

Ryleigh nods. "We'd love to."

She hops into her car and follows me home. It's easier than transferring the car seat to my car in the freezing cold weather. When I glance back at her ancient rusty sedan, I make a mental note to buy her a new car. Something safer, more reliable. Ryleigh won't like it, and that thought makes me smile. Twisted, I know.

I guess I'd just gotten used to being taken advantage of, and the fact that this woman couldn't care less about my fame or fortune blindsided me. Her sass and attitude about being independent makes me smile. Jesus, having her and a baby in my house at the same time makes me smile. I may have gotten in over my head—but damn, I know it'll be worth every second.

Back at my place, we unpack the diaper bag and I survey the guest room.

"We need to get a real crib," I say, watching as Ryleigh puts Ella down into the Pack 'n Play.

"You really want us to stay here?" she asks, her eyes wide and locked onto mine.

I stroke her cheek with my thumb. "I really want you to stay here. The place felt empty when you left. I slept for about four minutes last night." I don't remind her that the location of her run-down apartment makes me nervous. It's not safe for them there. I'll do everything in my power to make sure they don't have to go back.

"I—I guess we could try it . . ."

"Yeah?" My grin is huge as she lifts those blue eyes to mine, smiling.

"Yeah," she says.

"Okay, then. I think it's time to go shopping and set up a real baby nursery."

I grab my laptop from the counter and we settle onto the couch together, browsing the baby sites for the items we'll need. Ryleigh looks ready for a fight when I whip out my credit card, but I plant a big kiss on her lips to quiet her. It works perfectly. I'll have to remember that trick anytime she attempts to give me some of that sass. Keeps her quiet and I get to kiss her. Win-win.

We bought a matching crib and dresser, bedding, an upholstered rocking chair, and a furry pink rug for the floor in front of the crib that Ryleigh seemed to like.

Later, after a dinner of steak and potatoes that she prepares for us, we give Ella a bath together and put her to bed for the night. It feels oddly domestic, but somehow right.

I'm flipping through my team's playbook on the couch when Ryleigh joins me in the living room.

"Hey, there," she purrs. She's changed into her pajamas already, and I smile as I watch her approach. I love that she's so comfortable here.

I set down the playbook and turn to face her. "Don't freak out," I say as she settles in beside me.

"What are you talking about?"

"I made some calls. A friend of mine's wife owns a childcare center, a little preschool in a wealthy suburb about twenty minutes away. He said they're hiring for a preschool teacher. The pay is good, probably not as good as what you were making at the club, but there are full benefits, and you can bring Ella with you to work. She can go into the infant program."

Tears well in her eyes, and she blinks several

times. "I . . . I don't know what to say."

"Say yes." I smile.

"Yes."

T*hank God.*

Knowing she won't have to go back to that place ever again, won't ever be propositioned by sleazy men outside her building after work, is *huge.* The tension I've been carrying in my shoulders unknots, and I let out a heavy exhale. *What a relief.*

"And with you working a normal schedule, you can finish your teaching degree. I looked into some online programs for you."

Ryleigh brings her hands to my face, cupping my scruffy cheeks with her palms. "You big, bossy, crazy man."

I smile and lean down to press my lips against hers, resting my hand around the back of her neck. "I couldn't let you go. Not that easily. Ella really clinched the deal for me wanting you to stick around, ya know. Well, that and the amazing food and sex."

She grins again. "Are you done being bossy?"

"Not even a little."

She chuckles, and the sound is amazing.

I love seeing her like this, happy and carefree. There are still a lot of hard times ahead, including the awfulness of losing Andi and adjusting to parenthood. None of it will be easy, which is why we need to savor the good times even more. I intend to show her how to do exactly that.

"Come here, baby." I haul her onto my lap, and Ryleigh giggles when I tug her close. "I'm so glad you came back. And I'm so damn glad you agreed to take Ella. That was a very brave thing to do."

"Kiss me," she whispers, and I do, a lot.

She shifts her hips so we're pressed even closer. The heat of her sex is right up against my growing cock.

"We had our first fight as a real couple—sort of—so does that mean we're about to have make-up sex?" I grip her ass in both hands. *God, I can't get enough of her.* I pray she says yes.

Ryleigh smiles as she leans down and kisses me some more, still rocking her hips in a way that's killing me as she runs her hands through my hair. "Take me to bed and let's make up," she murmurs.

I carry her into my room—scratch that, *our* room—and take my time stripping her of her shirt, pants, and panties. When she's bare, I kiss every square inch of her from the delicate column of her throat to her full breasts, down to her stomach, until I reach the juncture between her thighs.

"Alexei . . ." She moans, fisting her hands in my hair as I taste her.

"You're perfect," I murmur, kissing her inner thigh.

Only once I've coaxed an orgasm from her body do I lie down next to her. Then I spoon my chest against her back, wrapping her tightly in my arms. She parts her thighs, inviting me in, and I enter her from behind. It's heaven to hold her like this and take her at the same time. I kiss the back of her neck as Ryleigh begins to work her hips against me.

"Yes, baby. Fuck." I pump my hips harder, my eyes falling closed.

"Alexei."

"That's it," I say, bringing one hand between us to rub her slick flesh. "Come for me."

A few moments more and she does, her body clenching wildly around mine until I groan and follow her over the edge.

CHAPTER
Sixteen

Alexei

"You can't be serious." I shoot a look at Ryleigh, and she rolls her eyes.

God, she looks beautiful tonight. She's wearing a little black dress and bright red lipstick. I secretly love that she's made such an effort for our date night.

She leans forward, placing her elbows on the table. "What? It'll be good, I'm sure."

"No way. No fucking way I'm letting you order just a salad at an Italian restaurant known for their homemade pasta."

She chuckles at me, shaking her head. We're on our first real date in what feels like an eternity, having gotten my mom to watch Ella, which wasn't difficult since she begs to see her almost daily.

Ryleigh and I have been living together for two months, and things have been perfect. It hasn't always been easy, but we're learning to navigate the rough patches together. She and Ella even traveled with me to my away game last weekend since I couldn't stand the thought of not seeing them for forty-eight hours.

Ryleigh eventually relents and closes her menu. "Fine. Lobster fettucine."

I grin. "That's my girl. Go big or go home, baby."

She rolls her eyes and leans back in her seat. "You're going to make me fat."

I reach across the table and squeeze her hand. "Not a chance. I love your curves."

The server comes and takes our orders. I can see the diners at the table beside us have spotted me and know who I am. I smile politely and tip my head, hoping they won't come to our table and interrupt a rare date out with Ryleigh. But knowing me, since I'm grateful for my career and fans, I'll sign their autographs without complaint if they do walk over.

To my agent's surprise, my relationship with Ryleigh hasn't caused the distraction Slate anticipated. If anything, Ryleigh's brought a sense of order to my life. Along with a whole lot of happiness and love that wasn't there before. There are no more fights with journalists or headlines about me losing my cool on some asshole. There's just me and my girls.

Andi is in her final days, and we bring Ella to the hospital often where Andi strokes her hair or holds her frail hand. I never imagined she'd have such a sense of peace, but seeing the way Ryleigh and I care for her, I know she's comforted knowing her daughter will be in good hands after she's gone. I even hired a photographer to come with us last time, photographing Andi and Ella together— a memento that Ella will hopefully treasure when she's much older and able to understand the sacrifice her mother made for her.

"I love that you don't have a game this weekend. It's nice having you home," Ryleigh says, taking a sip of her wine.

"It's the best. Just wait until the off-season. You'll be sick of me."

She shakes her head. "I highly doubt that."

Our food is delivered, and we waste no time digging in. I love how comfortable we are together. There are no awkward silences or need for pretense. I steal a bite of her pasta, and Ryleigh almost stabs me with her fork.

I chuckle and shake my head at her.

Ryleigh has been working at the preschool for a couple of weeks now, and it's been the perfect fit. She loves it and does an amazing job. And she's on track to finish her degree in about eighteen months, which will open up even more opportunities to her, if she wants.

"So, are you feeling ready for the playoffs?" Ryleigh asks, forking a bite of her pasta.

"Hell yes. With you by my side, baby, there's nothing I can't do."

She laughs, rolling her eyes at my cheesy line. "Think your mom will keep Ella for another hour?" she asks, her voice going sultry.

I smirk. "Yeah. Why, what did you have in mind?" The flirty look she's giving me makes me wonder if she's thinking about a lot more than dessert.

"I was thinking I'd like some uninterrupted sex

to top off our date."

I raise my hand, signaling to the server. "Check, please!"

Ryleigh chuckles.

A little while later we're back home, and we barely make it through the door before my lips are on Ryleigh's neck and I'm pressing her body up against the wall.

She lets out a murmured groan of approval, and I lift her so she can wrap her legs around my waist. I'm already hard for her, and I know she feels it, because she begins working her hips over my cock in a way that makes my balls ache.

"Shit, baby. Want you so bad."

"Yes, Alexei."

I work my hands beneath her dress and push her panties aside, stroking her wet, silky flesh while she makes a pleasure-filled sound of need.

I know I should take Ryleigh to the bedroom and lay her down against the pillows, make sure she's comfortable, and worship her like the goddess she is, but I'm far too impatient. And way too needy.

"Foreplay later? Need you now," I grunt as she palms my cock through my jeans and rubs it with her hand.

She makes a noise of agreement, and I work open the front of my jeans and shove them down over my ass with one hand until my cock is free. And then I push into Ryleigh's tight body, stroking her inner walls until she's panting and moaning and clawing at my shoulders.

"It feels so good, Alexei."

I kiss her mouth once and then meet her eyes. "Yeah, baby?"

I pump my hips in a lazy rhythm, loving that I'm driving her wild with desire. Her eyes are hooded, and her head is resting against the wall as she watches me. I'm in no rush to end this, and continue pushing into her in long, slow strokes as I watch her cheeks blush and her eyes go hazy with lust.

"Tell me. Let me hear you."

"I love your big cock. Give it to me," she says on a moan, gripping me tighter.

Her words do something to me, and heat blooms in my chest. But rather than respond to her dirty endearment, as amazing as it was, I'm hungry for more.

My hips are still moving, but only barely. I take a deep breath and meet her eyes. "I love *you*."

Ryleigh's eyes widen at my words. It's the first time I've told her how I feel, but definitely not the first time I've wanted to. I've known how I feel about her for weeks now. Shit, if I'm being honest, I think I knew that first night.

Her grip around my shoulders tightens, and her eyes grow watery. She looks so beautiful like this—so full of love, so full of me.

"I love you too." Her voice is barely above a whisper, but there's so much emotion behind her words. I sense she's been waiting for some time to say that to me.

Welcome to the club, sweetheart.

Her words release something in me, and I begin fucking her hard and fast against the wall. Ryleigh cries out, gripping me as I pummel into her, our bodies melding together perfectly. Soon, she climaxes, clenching wildly around me as she says my name over and over. I love the sound of it on her lips. I love everything about her. Her strength, her stubbornness, and best of all—the fact that she's mine.

"Jeez, Alexei." She sighs when I finally lower her to her feet inside our bedroom. It's dark, but I don't bother with the lights. She's still clutching my biceps like she doesn't quite trust herself to be steady on her feet just yet.

"You okay, baby?" I lean down and press a soft kiss to her forehead.

She nods quickly, tucking her hair behind one ear. "I'd say I'm much better than okay."

I chuckle. "Yeah. That was . . ." Truthfully? There are no words. I just get so worked up when I'm around her. I've never felt like this with a woman before. It's like no matter how many times I have her, rather than satisfy my hunger, I only end up wanting her more. "You're incredible. I'm sorry that wasn't more romantic."

Our first fucking date night in forever, and I practically maul her, and then fuck her in the hall-way up against a wall. *Shit. What's wrong with me?*

Though I can't regret telling her I love her. I do, so fucking much.

She rolls her eyes. "So much for foreplay."

I squeeze her ass and chuckle. "I didn't hear

you complaining. And . . ." I give her a wicked smirk.

"What?" She laughs, somewhat nervously.

"Your pussy was really wet."

She swats at my bicep. "Oh my God, Alexei!"

I laugh again, leaning down to kiss her. "Next time, more foreplay. Got it. I promise."

She shakes her head at me, but she's still grinning.

"I meant what I said, though," I add.

She cocks her head, watching me as I pull up my jeans and button them. "About what?"

I take her face in my hands. "That I love you."

And I do. It's fast, but I've never felt more sure about anything in my entire life. She makes me smile and gives my heart this full, happy feeling. Plus she turns me on more than any woman ever has.

Her cheeks blush, and she looks almost shy. She didn't think it was only something we were going to say in the heat of the moment, did she? That's not how I roll. I wouldn't have said it if it wasn't 100 percent true.

After just a moment's hesitation, she seems to find her footing. "I love you too."

I break into a happy grin. "Good. Now get dressed so we can go get our baby."

Ryleigh giggles as she grabs one of my T-shirts and puts it on.

CHAPTER
Seventeen

Ryleigh

Two Months Later

Oh my God, I had no idea watching Alexei on the football field from my spot in the suite would be so incredibly stressful. I stand here, gripping the seat in front of me, my gaze glued to him on the field. My stomach is in knots and my palms are sweating.

I'm wearing the jersey Alexei bought me in his team colors—navy and gold—with his number embroidered on the back. Most of the wives and girlfriends in the suite are dressed similarly, and some even have the word WIFEY printed across the back of their jerseys. It's cute, and I wonder briefly if I'll ever have one like that. The thought of it makes my belly tighten.

I almost brought Ella tonight, but now I'm glad I listened to Tracey's advice and left her with Alexei's mom at home. I'm sure Irina is glued to the TV, watching the big game.

Alexei's three sisters are on their feet cheering, yelling out curses and encouragements that may as well be in a different language. It's obvious they grew up around the game, and they know all the terminology that I don't. Or maybe some of it is in Russian, who the hell knows. Nothing would surprise me with this family.

The only thing I know is that our team is down by three points, and it's the final seconds of the game. And not just any game, but the big championship game that will determine the national champs.

Yeah, my stomach is in knots, to say the least. I'm so nervous and excited and anxious for Alexei.

"Get your fucking head out of your ass, Lex!" Tracey yells.

I'm sure he can't hear her from our spot inside the suite, but I shake my head at her. "What's going to happen now?" I don't know all the rules of the game as well as I should—clearly.

Tracey rolls her eyes. "Either he stops them from advancing on this next play, or they hand over their balls to the other team."

I nod. "Got it."

So it all comes down to this. The crowd around us quiets, and the entire stadium is glued to this moment.

I take a deep breath, holding it in my lungs, and say a silent prayer. *Come on, Alexei. You can do this. I know it.*

I watch with wide eyes as his team gathers into formation. When they break, Alexei's friend Weston Chase heaves the ball, his thick arm stretching as the ball releases, hurtling through the air in a perfect spiral.

My gaze returns to Alexei's hulking form. He's right in the middle of the pack, fighting off guys who are trying to advance toward the end line. It's so incredible to watch him—his sheer size and strength—and seeing this version of him shoving at men even bigger than he is, so different from the soft and gentle guy I get at home. I smile, enjoying watching my man at work.

The crowd around me erupts into cheers, and the sound is deafening. Alexei's sisters jump up and down, screaming, and it takes me a minute to understand what's happening.

Oh my God. We won.

"We won!" I scream.

Tracey laughs. "We fucking did it!"

"Booyah, yes!" Valerie cheers.

The team gathers around the coach, and then Alexei charges toward the sideline. On instinct, I rush out of the suite and toward the field. Alexei tugs off his helmet and shares a hug with Weston. They're shouting something to each other, and Weston is jumping up and down.

When Alexei sees me, his face breaks into a huge grin. He's sweaty and dirty, but I've never seen him happier.

"Baby! Get over here."

I rush into his arms, and we laugh and cry as we hug each other and kiss.

"You did it," I say, nearly having to shout. It's so loud in here.

"We did. I love you, baby."

"I love you too."

Alexei releases me and looks deeply into my eyes, cupping my face in his hands. He looks like he wants to say something, but instead, he drops to one knee in front of me. He takes my hands and nods to someone behind me.

Wait. What's happening?

Before I can process or question what's going on, Alexei looks up into my eyes and gives my hands a tender squeeze.

"I love you, baby. You and Ella. I want you to be mine. I want us to be a family. Forever. Will you marry me?"

Tears gather in my eyes. With all the commotion around us, his words barely register. People are still hugging and cheering and it's pure chaos, but the best kind of chaos. I realize a cameraman has stopped to film us—Alexei in his uniform and my stunned face are being plastered on every giant screen around the dome. And that's when it hits me.

"Oh my God, you're proposing?" I bring a trembling hand to my lips.

He smirks. "That was kind of the plan. Win the game. Get the girl. Live happily ever after."

Tears stream freely down my cheeks as I stare at him.

People are watching us. People in the stands, on the sidelines, Alexei's teammates, his sisters . . .

Still on one knee, he gives a nod to his oldest sister, Ana, who walks over and hands him something small. It takes me a minute to realize it's a ring, a beautiful diamond ring, and I've never seen a ring this pretty in my entire life. Alexei holds it up and meets my eyes.

I'm not sure if I expected him to pull the ring out of his tight uniform pants, but I'm sure those don't even have pockets. And dear God, you don't bring a ring like this onto a football field. It's massive. At least three carats, and so sparkly and gorgeous. My heart is beating way too fast, and I suck in a big gulp of air.

"What do you say, baby? Will you marry me?"

The loving look in his eyes as he watches me makes my knees weak. "Yes!" I shout, and he breaks into a huge grin.

Alexei slides the ring onto my shaking finger, and I try desperately to wipe away the tears with my free hand.

"This is too much," I say, admiring the way the bright lights catch the ring and make it shimmer.

He presses a kiss to my knuckles and then rises to his feet. "I wanted you to have the best."

"Bossy," I say, bringing my mouth to his.

The entire stadium erupts into cheers, almost even louder than when the team scored the winning touchdown. My heart feels so full and happy, it could burst. Alexei sweeps me up into his arms and kisses me—really kisses me, devouring my mouth like no one is watching—and I melt into him. The cheers grow even louder, and we finally break apart, laughing.

"You need a shower," I say, patting his butt.

"Come with me." His eyes are mischievous and bright.

I chuckle. "I don't think so."

"Fine. Wait for me?" he asks.

"Always."

He presses one last quick kiss to my lips before hugging each of his sisters. I watch him walk away toward the locker room with some of his teammates, who are patting him on the back and congratulating him. I can't help but think about his mother, who likely just watched the entire proposal on TV.

His sisters pull me into a group hug, and Valerie, the youngest, is crying she's so happy. It's beyond sweet. I haven't felt part of a family in so long that tears spring to my own eyes again.

I can't even imagine what my life would be like right now if Alexei hadn't stopped that night on the street—if he hadn't intervened with that guy outside the club. I shudder when I picture it.

"Alexei! Wait!" I call, jogging over to where he stands at the edge of the field before he heads to the locker room.

He turns and sees the emotion written all over my face. I run straight into his arms and plaster my face against his neck. He lifts me and I wrap my legs around him, clinging to his muscular frame like he's my safety, my security, because he really is.

"Thank you. I love you so much."

He pulls back and cups my face with one hand. "I love you too. You and Ella. You're mine now, okay?"

"*Da.*" I nod.

He breaks into deep laughter, chuckling at my use of Russian. "You're the best. See you in a minute, okay? I promise I won't smell so bad when I come back out."

"You know I don't mind your smell, but yes, I'll be waiting with your sisters."

"They're your sisters now too."

A fresh wave of emotion hits, and my throat feels tight. "See you in a minute."

I rejoin his sisters—my sisters—in the suite, where they promptly all lose their minds over how stunning my ring is. I have never felt happier or more loved in my entire life, and I never want this feeling to end.

Epilogue

Alexei

Five years later . . .

"I don't think I can do this," Ryleigh whispers from the passenger side of the car, her hand resting on the round bump of her belly.

My stomach drops, and I reach over and place my hand on her knee. I hate the thought that she's scared. "The glucose test? It'll be fine. It's just a quick blood draw. I'll hold your hand and distract you. Anything you need."

She rolls her eyes and shakes her head at me. "I'm not talking about the glucose test today."

She's six months pregnant with our second

daughter, our first biological child, if you want to get technical about it. Either way, I'm over the fucking moon. We're headed to the doctor's office after we drop Ella off at her first day of kindergarten. So, yeah, it's a big day all around.

Ryleigh's gaze darts to the back seat where Ella sits, humming quietly to herself. "I mean . . . did we really consider homeschooling, because it's not too late, you know?"

I swallow a chuckle and stare straight ahead as the parking attendant at the private school we've selected for Ella motions us forward into the drop-off line. "Baby, this is one of the best schools in the entire country. Ella is going to love it."

Ella's been talking about her first day of kindergarten for months. She's ready—even if Ryleigh's not.

Ryleigh completed her master's degree in teaching last year, and she would have been teaching here this year if she hadn't gotten pregnant. She decided to take one more year at home, knowing it was Ella's last year at home too. But they held her position and she'll begin teaching first grade next year when the baby is about eight months old. Though to be honest, I really wonder how long that will last. My mother is determined that she'll be the one watching the baby, but I have my doubts that Ryleigh will really want to leave the baby and go back to work.

I'll support whatever she wants to do, of course. God knows with my salary, she certainly doesn't have to work. The Hawks renewed my contract for another three years—another $30 million. After that, I plan to retire. Retired by thirty-six sounds about right to me. Then I can enjoy all of my girls more. No more early morning practices or away games. I'm already looking forward to it, although Ryleigh swears I'll miss it. I may miss the game, but I won't miss being away from them on such a grueling schedule.

More time with the ones I love is not something I take for granted. Especially after watching Andi struggle and die so young. To be fair though, Andi exceeded all expectations, living until Ella was nine months old, crawling around, babbling, and saying Dada. She loved her daughter, and loved how happy the baby made Ryleigh and me. I know she's in a better place, and Ryleigh and I made peace a long time ago with her passing. Plus, we got the best gift in the entire world—Ella. Which brings us to this moment.

"I don't know, Alexei." Ryleigh chews on her

lower lip, eyeing the sturdy brick building.

"Mommy, is that my school?" Ella asks from the back seat, her voice chipper. Thankfully, she's completely oblivious to Ryleigh's near breakdown.

"That's your school, my love. What do you think?" I ask as Ryleigh wipes at her teary eyes with a tissue.

"Yay!" Ella cheers.

I chuckle, and even Ryleigh lets out a small, sad laugh.

Pregnancy suits her. She's still petite and beautiful as ever, but with full breasts and a round tummy that even strangers can't seem to help but reach out and touch. Of course, she's more emotional than she's ever been, which I'm still learning how to navigate.

"You okay?" I press my hand to her knee once again and give it a squeeze.

She gives me a brave nod, swallowing the lump in her throat. "I guess I have to be." Leaning around the passenger seat, she looks back at Ella, reaching out to smooth her hair where it's been so neatly braided. "Why did you have to grow up so fast, love?"

Ella giggles. "Because, Mommy! I'm a big girl."

"I know you are. I'm so proud of you. Go have an amazing first day of kindergarten. We'll pick you up at the end of the day."

"Daddy too?"

Ryleigh nods. "Daddy too."

"Listen to your teacher, okay?" I say, giving Ella our secret double wink. She repeats it back to me, rapidly blinking both eyes.

"I will, Daddy!"

Hearing her sweet voice call me daddy never gets old. I chuckle as she unbuckles her own seat belt and climbs out of the car with her brightly colored unicorn lunch box.

She looks so small following the teacher up the sidewalk and into the building. Fucking hell. Tears fill my eyes as I watch her walk away and a lump the size of Illinois lodges in my throat.

"See. Told ya this sucks," Ryleigh says, wiping away the fresh tears that are falling from her eyes when she notices my watery eyes.

"Fucking sucks. Big time," I say, putting the

car into drive and pulling away reluctantly. "What time is school over?"

"Two o'clock."

This is going to be the longest six hours of my life.

• • •

"Have you guys decided on a name yet?" my agent, Slate, asks, grabbing a bottle of water from the ice bucket on the counter.

It's several nights later, and Ryleigh and I are hosting a small dinner party at our new-ish apartment in an exclusive gated neighborhood downtown. We decided we needed a little more space before the baby came. My old bachelor pad was fine for Ryleigh, Ella, and me, but that had ran its course.

Two months ago, we moved into this place, which is a few miles closer to Ella's new school. We have a beautiful terrace overlooking the city and four thousand square feet, which is plenty big enough for all the baby dolls and Legos that currently decorate our space.

Tonight, we're hosting a small dinner party for our close friends. Slate is here with his wife, Keaton, and their six-month-old son, Beckham. So are Weston and Jane and their daughter and their twin boys—aka their hellions, who totally fucking take after Weston. Which sucks. For Jane. They just turned three, and yeah, I'm surprised they haven't started a fire or killed each other by now. After being around them, I wouldn't wish twins on my worst enemy. Beau and Bennett are fair-haired like Jane but built like Weston—bulky and too tall for their age, and extremely physical. Ella adores their daughter Madison, but she's visiting her grandparents tonight.

The only other people missing from the party are our good friends Cam and Natalie. They are in Hawaii for a destination wedding for their friends Jack and Meredith, but it's probably just as well. They are our only friends without kids, and being around all this chaos might deter them from procreating. But ever since they got married last year, all they've talked about is babies, so I know it's not far off for them.

Realizing that Slate is still waiting for my reply, I shake my head. "We're still figuring that out. We have a list."

Slate chuckles. "Oh, I remember the list."

Keaton elbows him. "You loved my list."

Slate gives her a crooked grin. "You mean your spreadsheet with the color-coded tabs."

Keaton, his wife and more analytical half, chuckles. "Yes. That. It was genius."

"That it was," Slate says.

"Our list is a little less sophisticated. It's on an old takeout napkin taped to the side of the fridge."

Ryleigh's eyes meet mine, and her hand rests on her stomach. "We'll figure it out. We have time."

Jane nods and leads Ryleigh into the living room toward the couch. "You have plenty of time. We didn't name the twins until they were three days old."

After I check on the meal, I join the gang in the living room and settle on the couch beside Ryleigh.

Ella, the only little girl amongst the little kids, clearly rules the roost. They're playing babies. Beau and Bennett each hold a naked baby doll in their lap as Ella gives them instructions on how to diaper them. I grin as I watch. Beside me, Weston frowns.

"Might need to get them some baby dolls," I say.

Weston shrugs. "Jane already has. Something about gender-neutral toys."

I nod. "Guess it makes sense. For her first birth-day, I got Ella a football."

"Along with full tackle gear," Ryleigh adds, rolling her eyes.

"Didn't Ella have her first day of kindergarten this week?" Jane asks. "How did that go?"

"Ugh. Awful." Ryleigh shakes her head. "A piece of advice . . . don't let them grow up."

"Are you sure?" Slate asks. "Because I'd kind of like to go back to sleeping through the night. That'd be fucking awesome."

Keaton elbows him again. "I told you not to get up every time he needs his pacifier. We need to sleep-train him." She ruffles the fuzzy brown curls on her baby son's head as he sits perched on her knee, watching the older children play.

"Ella loves school, loves her teacher," Ryleigh says. "But yeah, Alexei and I were both in tears when we watched her walk inside."

I scoff. "I was not in tears." I just had a little something in my eye is all.

Weston chuckles. "The big bad linebacker crying at school drop-off. What a puss—I mean, what a baby."

Jabbing him in the side with my elbow, I glare at him. "Just wait until your twins start school, fucker," I whisper, low enough that Weston hears me but the innocent little ears don't.

Jane perks up, sitting up straighter. "Well, I for one can't wait for that day. The three hours a day the twins are at preschool is like heaven."

Ryleigh chuckles and pats Jane's hand. "You deserve a break, Mama."

Isn't that the damn truth? Those twins are crazy, but I don't say as much. I just nod in agreement with Ryleigh. It is pretty incredible how captivated the boys are by Ella. They haven't overturned a potted plant or started a fire in my microwave yet this visit. Turns out, if you nuke an iPhone, the fucker will explode into flames. Who knew?

The timer beeps in the kitchen, signaling that dinner is ready, and I rise to my feet. "Dinner in five, guys."

After cleaning up the baby dolls and their accessories, Ryleigh makes a little assembly line, helping the children wash their hands before dinner.

I place two large casserole pans of lasagna in the center of the table, along with a huge salad and two overflowing bread baskets. Everyone takes their seats, with baby Beckham in Ella's old high chair between Slate and Keaton. Ella and the twins are at a tiny version of our mahogany dining table that I had made for her. Ryleigh is by my side, and Weston and Jane sit across from us.

"This looks great, Alex," Jane says, setting prepared plates in front of the twins and rejoining us at the table.

I can't help but notice the line in Ryleigh's forehead. Anytime someone calls me Alex, it still seems to throw her off. I smile at her, and when she notices, she grins at me. Her smile is bright and uninhibited, so happy, it almost takes my breath away.

Once the food is dished up and everyone has dug in, I place a hand on Ryleigh's knee under the table and give it a gentle squeeze.

"I love you," I murmur, leaning in closer.

She looks at me, meeting my eyes with a half smile on her lips. "I love you too," she whispers, leaning closer.

"Forever?" I ask, grinning.

"And ever," she replies, and my heart swells.

I reach over and place my hand on the firm curve of her belly. Sometimes I try to picture how my life would be if she and Ella hadn't come bursting into it. These aren't pleasant thoughts. It's a sad and lonely existence where I'm still single and struggling to find myself in the world. It's a place where football is my entire life, and honestly, it sounds so sad to me now that I almost hate to picture it. My life was so empty before.

Even though Ryleigh thinks I'll miss it and be miserable, I can't wait to retire from football after this contract ends. More time with my girls sounds exactly perfect. I have plans to buy a vacation home on the beach somewhere, and sleep late and make epic pancake breakfasts . . . there are so many things I'm looking forward to. But none more than loving and protecting my girls for all my days on this earth.

"Pass the salad?" Keaton asks, snapping me from my daydream.

I hand her the salad bowl, grateful that we have such wonderful friends we can count on.

"You okay there?" Ryleigh asks, smirking at

me. She clearly noticed the fact that I was deep in thought.

"Never better," I say with a grin, but I'm lying.

It's hard to imagine, but I know I'll be even better when we have a new baby in the house. After all, I am the baby-whisperer.

• • •

Thank you so much for reading *Finding Alexei*! I truly hope you loved this story as much as I do.

I started this journey with Keaton and Slate, one of my favorite couples ever, in *Love Machine*. Cam and Natalie followed in *Flirting with Forever*, and Weston and Jane came next in *Dear Jane*. I hope you read about them all, but if not, I would encourage you to go check them out!

I had a blast writing this series. Each story is a standalone, but I really do hope that you will enjoy each and every one. You deserve it, girl.

Love,

Kendall

Acknowledgments

Thank you so much to my incredible readers. I hope you enjoyed this story. Every reader deserves a hot hero and a happy ending! And I had a blast writing about an alpha male with a soft spot for babies, so there's that. I'm so grateful to my team—Pam, Karen, Elaine, Becca, Alyssa, Anthony, Flavia, Danielle . . . I am so blessed to have your guidance.

Other Books in This Series

If you liked *Finding Alexei*, you will also want to pick up the related books in this series— *Love Machine*, about Alexei's sports agent, Slate; *Flirting with Forever*, featuring Cam and Natalie; and *Dear Jane*, featuring Alexei's teammate Weston. Check out the synopses for all three books that follow. I think you would really enjoy them all!

LOVE machine

She says she needs some help . . . in the bed-room.

Come again? No, really *come again.*

Sweet, nerdy, lovable Keaton.

She's my best friend and has been for years. Sure, she likes numbers and math, and thinks doing other people's taxes is fun. And I like . . . none of that stuff. She's obsessed with her cat and reads novels I'll never understand, and yet we just click. There's no one I'd rather share breakfast burritos with or binge watch hours of Netflix. She's my person. And so when she takes off her glasses and asks me to help her improve her skills in the bedroom, I barely have to think about it.

Of course I'll help her. There's no one better for the job.

I've been there for her through everything, so why should this be any different?

But what happens when she's ready to take her newfound confidence and move on?

FLIRTING WITH *Forever*

No women.

No sex.

No hooking up.

This is the oath I took in solidarity with my best friend after a particularly heinous breakup left him shattered.

No problem, right?

Wrong.

Because lately I've begun developing big, messy feelings for our best female friend who we both swore was off-limits since we were sixteen years old.

I shouldn't notice the way her hair turns golden when it catches the light, and I shouldn't make it a goal to see her dimples when she laughs.

I'm pretty sure she's oblivious, which is a good thing, I try to convince myself.

Until one night after too many cocktails when

we fall into bed together. I'm left with an awkward morning-after, and one of the hardest choices I've ever had to make.

Confess how I feel, and potentially lose both of my best friends in the process, or bury my feelings and watch her move on?

How can something so wrong feel so right?

DEAR

I broke her heart ten years ago and left town.

She hates me, and rightly so. It doesn't matter that the rest of the country loves me, that I'm a starting quarterback with a multimillion-dollar contract. Because when I look in the mirror, all I see is a failure who was too young—and too afraid—to fight for what I wanted.

But I'm not that guy anymore, and all I need is one shot to convince her.

• • •

He has no idea what happened after he left. And now I'm supposed to work alongside him like we don't have this huge, messy history?

But I'm older now, wiser, and I won't let anything stand in my way of doing a good job for this league. Not even one overpaid, arrogant player who thinks we're going to kiss and make up.

News flash, buddy: I am over you.

Get Two Free Books

Sign up for my newsletter and I'll automatically send you two free books.

www.kendallryanbooks.com/newsletter

What to Read Next

Boyfriend for hire

I'm the guy you call when you need to impress your overbearing family, your boss, or your ex. Yeah, I'm a male escort, but not just any escort, I'm the escort. The one with a mile-long waiting list and a pristine reputation that's very well-deserved.

I'm the guy who'll make you feel beautiful, desired, and worshipped . . . all for a steep price. I'm hired to make you shine, and I always deliver.

I'll be whatever you want me to be for one night—except my true self. This is just a job, a role I play to earn a paycheck.

But I'm not the guy who falls for a client. Not once in six years.

And then I meet Elle. Her friend has hired me to escort her to a wedding, but Elle doesn't know we're just pretending.

There's a fire between us I never expected. A connection I haven't felt in so long. One kiss, and I'm losing all control.

But what will happen when she finds out who I really am?

Boyfriend

for hire

Sneak Preview

Chapter One

Nic

I pull up outside the mini-mansion and check my reflection in the mirror. Dressed in a tailored black suit with a crisp white shirt, I know I look good . . . actually, better than good. It's not being cocky if it's true, and I was blessed with good genetics. That's just a fact of life.

After closing the visor, I slip my sunglasses inside my jacket pocket and climb from my shiny black Tesla, ready to get on with my workday.

I let myself inside and head through the marble foyer of Case's home. He runs the Allure agency out of his home office, but this place is so large, I swear he doesn't even notice that at any given time there are at least two or three guys hanging out here, eating his food, drinking his beer, or using his home gym. It's basically become a male-escort headquarters in an unsuspecting neighborhood in an upscale suburb of Chicago.

Inside, I find Ryder, Case's right hand and best friend . . . and a fellow escort.

"Hey, dude," I say. It's just after five, and Ryder's sitting on the couch with a beer in his hand. Doesn't he have to work later too? It's probably not a good sign, but who am I to judge?

"What's up, man?" Ryder says, his gaze still on the football game playing on TV.

"Just stopping by to see Case. Is he in his office?" Even if I haven't seen him yet, I know Case is home. His Mercedes is parked outside.

Ryder grunts something that I think means *yes*, and I head down the hall.

Ryder is playful, fun-loving, and cocky as fuck. Women love him with his bright blue eyes and lightly tanned skin. He's like a walking fantasy with his square jawline and preppy clothes. And the motherfucker's calendar proves it. He's even busier than Case, which is saying something.

Even if Case and Ryder seem happy enough, I

know I don't want to end up like them. I don't plan to be a lifer. I'll make money escorting, and then hopefully move on to something else.

Part of me can't believe I've lasted six years doing this. When I met Case and he offered me a job, I scoffed at the idea and blew him off. Then he told me how much I could make—five grand a night—and explained that I wouldn't necessarily have to sleep with anyone for money.

So I said *fuck it* and decided to give it a shot.

I've slept with women I haven't necessarily wanted to sleep with for free, so this is a no-brainer. I figured I'd do it once or twice, take my money, and be done with it.

But the truth is, I couldn't find a job that would even come close to matching this kind of income, and it's spoiled me a bit. Getting to wine and dine beautiful women for a living? It's not exactly a hardship, and even if it were, I'd gladly take one for the team.

Case opened Allure a couple of years before he hired me, and he hasn't slowed down or taken a day off in all that time. The guy's a machine. Tall and commanding, he's able to blend into any social situation with ease. It's a gift, really. Most of the time he's dressed in a suit, but today I find him in a pair of gym shorts and a T-shirt sitting in front of his laptop.

He's as comfortable wining and dining a cougar in a five-star restaurant as he is hanging with us on his couch in sweatpants, scarfing down day-old pizza. Actually, I've looked up to him for a long time. He runs his business with zero drama, pays his taxes, and is able to employ a half dozen of his best friends. It's a pretty sweet deal.

"Hey, what's up?" he asks when he spots me lingering in the doorway to his office.

"Just came to check my schedule for the week."

His gaze lifts from the laptop screen and he smirks. "Yeah, about that. Sit, would you?"

As I sink into the leather chair in front of his desk, an uneasy feeling settles in the pit of my stomach.

"So, I know you're booked with Rebecca from six to nine tonight."

I nod. I met Rebecca three months ago, and now she's a regular. She's an easy client to entertain. As a recently divorced attorney, she has little time for dating, and so twice a month, I fill that void. We go to dinner, and then back to her place where we have vanilla sex. All in all, it's not a hard evening for me. And I leave several grand richer.

"Well, Donovan called in sick tonight. So, after Rebecca, you're meeting Amy at nine thirty. A hotel downtown. I'll text you the address."

I run a hand through my hair and let out a sigh. Entertaining two women in one evening isn't the ideal scenario. "Isn't there someone else?"

Case shakes his head. "Ryder and I are both booked too. Think you can handle a doubleheader?"

I know what he's really asking. Will I be able to get it up and deliver twice within as many hours? "That won't be a problem. But what do you know about Amy?"

Case's firm mouth softens. "You'll like her. Thirty-something, fit, and attractive. She's a single mom who occasionally books with Donovan or Ryder to blow off some steam."

I nod. It's not like I have much of a choice. "Fine."

"Thanks, man." Case looks down at his desk, seeming preoccupied.

"Is that all?" Why do I get the feeling there's something else?

He smirks again. "I know I told you that you'd have tomorrow off, but . . ."

I bite the inside of my cheek. I've been looking forward to sleeping in late tomorrow, hitting the gym, and then spending the afternoon at my apartment's rooftop pool to relax. I've been working too much lately as it is.

"But what?" I ask.

Case leans forward on his elbows. "There's a woman I need you to meet. It's just coffee. Fifteen minutes, tops."

"What's the situation. Why coffee?"

"Guess she wants to meet you before she commits. It happens sometimes," he says with a shrug, then closes his laptop and rises to his feet. "It'll be your job to make her feel comfortable, win her over."

I let out a sigh and stand. "Fine."

Case hands me a sheet of paper that outlines my appointments for the rest of the week. Weekends are busiest, but I still have one or two clients I entertain midweek. I fold the paper and place it inside my jacket pocket, along with my sunglasses.

Since it's almost time to get my evening started, I head out, saying good-bye to Case and then Ryder on my way out.

I really do love my job.

>>—♡—→

Two hours later, I grab the small black duffel bag I keep in my car for work and start up the walk after Rebecca. It contains all the basics—condoms, lube, a variety of vibrators, a silk blindfold, baby wipes, my toothbrush, and a small stash of Viagra.

I've needed help a couple of times to get hard for a client, but thankfully it doesn't happen often. I love sex, and usually the women who book me are attractive socialite types who are bored of their husband and can afford to spend his money on a younger model.

At first, this bothered me—a lot, actually—but then I realized their husbands were doing the same thing—out seeing women half their age, sleeping with their secretaries on the side, basically nailing anything they could catch and release. Once I realized this was the way the game is played in their world, I got along just fine. That isn't to say that sometimes I don't like the feeling of being a pawn in their game. Even if I do support a woman taking charge of her own pleasure, there's still the stigma.

I'd like to think I provide a valuable service. A forty-five-year-old client once told me that she'd never had an orgasm with her husband in twenty-two years of marriage. That's some sad shit right there. I guess this job is just me making up for in-adequate men who can't please their ladies. Need-less to say, she came four times that first night with me, and continued booking me on and off for over a year until she worked up the courage to ask her husband for a divorce. When she remarried last year, I was invited to her wedding. I didn't go— that would have been weird—but I did send her a toaster. And it was a nice fucking toaster, if I do say so myself.

Dinner with Rebecca is nice, uneventful, and the conversation pleasant. Rebecca always pays, and we always eat at her favorite restaurant, an American bistro with big juicy steaks. Not that I've ever tried one. While I'm working, I try to eat light, knowing the aerobic activities I'll be engaging in later in the evening.

Rebecca shimmies her hips as she walks, her round ass filling out her black pencil skirt nicely. I smirk as I watch her. *No need to seduce me, sweetheart. I'll be fucking you tonight no matter what.*

When she unlocks the door and lets us inside, I'm familiar enough with her fantasies by now that I barely wait for her to close the door behind us. Pressing her against the wall, I devour her neck with kisses.

I never kiss on the mouth, but I have no problem putting my mouth pretty much anywhere else. Well, not *anywhere*. I don't do oral. It's one of the rules I've set for myself. There's something about it that's just so intimate, I'd prefer to save it for someone who means something to me. But Rebecca's interests are pretty tame. She just wants to feel desired. Wants to feel that a man is so enamored with her that he can barely wait until they're inside the bedroom to have her. It's a fantasy I'm happy to act out for her.

I cup her round ass in my palms and give it a squeeze as my teeth nip at her exposed collarbone. It's all very practiced, even if it doesn't seem like it to her.

Her palms explore the contours of my chest beneath my suit jacket, and she makes a pleased sound low in her throat. "Yes, Nic."

My cock hardens as she whimpers and rubs her body against mine.

"Tell me what you want," I whisper against her neck.

Rebecca shivers. "You. My room. Now."

Her bedroom is always immaculately clean, and it smells faintly of lilacs. I waste no time in stripping her down to the black lacy lingerie she always wears for me, and then I'm in my boxer briefs and Rebecca is on her knees in front of me. Thankfully, I'm fully hard now.

While she's never asked me to return the favor, Rebecca usually likes our foreplay to include some time spent with my cock in her mouth. I'm not one to complain about this scenario.

"You're so sexy with my cock in your mouth," I murmur, stroking her hair as I close my eyes.

Thirty minutes later, Rebecca's come twice, and I'm pumping away, sweat dampening my lower back. I glance quickly at her bedside clock to check the time, deciding enough time has passed to allow myself to come. So I finally let go, filling the condom with a sharp exhale.

After a quick visit to the restroom, where I

freshen up and dress, I find Rebecca wrapped in her silk sheets, her hair mussed from sex and a satisfied smile on her lips.

"You sure you don't want to stay? I have gelato in my freezer." She grins like we're lovers who have just finished a real date . . . not an impersonal transaction where money exchanges hands.

I'm not sure whether to feel flattered or annoyed. I decide on flattered.

Leaning down to give her ass cheek a squeeze, I shake my head. "Wish I could, darling. I've got plans later."

She nods, her eyes bright and happy. A couple of orgasms will do that to a woman. "Okay. Good night then, Nic."

"Good night."

I release a sigh as I head back down the walk, duffel in hand, toward my car.

One down; one left to go tonight.

And tomorrow, on what's supposed to be my day off, Case has me working. Some coffee date. *At least it won't be sex* crosses my mind as I start the engine to head to appointment number two.

Jesus, what man in his right mind thinks "at least it won't be sex" without needing to visit a mental health professional for a complete check-up? I'm thinking I really need a day off.

Follow Kendall

BookBub has a feature where you can follow me and get an alert when I release a book or put a title on sale. Sign up here to stay in the loop:

www.bookbub.com/authors/kendall-ryan

Website

www.kendallryanbooks.com

Facebook

www.facebook.com/kendallryanbooks

Twitter

www.twitter.com/kendallryan1

Instagram

www.instagram.com/kendallryan1

Newsletter

www.kendallryanbooks.com/newsletter

About the Author

A *New York Times*, *Wall Street Journal*, and *USA TODAY* bestselling author of more than two dozen titles, Kendall Ryan has sold over two million books, and her books have been translated into several languages in countries around the world. Her books have also appeared on the *New York Times* and *USA TODAY* bestseller list more than three dozen times. Kendall has been featured in publications such as *USA TODAY*, *Newsweek*, and *In Touch Magazine*. She lives in Texas with her husband and two sons.

To be notified of new releases or sales, join Kendall's private Mailing List:

www.kendallryanbooks.com/newsletter

Get even more of the inside scoop when you join Kendall's private Facebook group, Kendall's Kinky Cuties:

www.facebook.com/groups/kendallskinkycuties

Other Books by Kendall Ryan

Unravel Me

Make Me Yours

Working It

Craving Him

All or Nothing

When I Break Series

Filthy Beautiful Lies Series

The Gentleman Mentor

Sinfully Mine

Bait & Switch

Slow & Steady

The Room Mate

The Play Mate

The House Mate

The Bed Mate

The Soul Mate

Hard to Love

Reckless Love

Resisting Her

The Impact of You

Screwed

Monster Prick

The Fix Up

Sexy Stranger

Dirty Little Secret

Dirty Little Promise

Torrid Little Affair

xo, Zach

Baby Daddy

Tempting Little Tease

Bro Code

Love Machine

Flirting with Forever

Dear Jane

For a complete list of Kendall's books, visit:
www.kendallryanbooks.com/all-books/

CPSIA information can be obtained
at www.ICGtesting.com
Printed in the USA
LVHW112103180719
624590LV00001B/138/P